PAROCHIAL PIGS

BOOK 1 IN THE PIGS TRILOGY

JAMES JENKINS

 URBAN PIGS PRESS

urbanpigspress.co.uk

First published by Alien Buddha Press 2021
Second Edition by Urban Pigs Press 2024
© 2021 James Jenkins
© ™®

All Rights Reserved. The moral rights of the author have been declared by the author as the owner of this work. Any reproduction in whole or part must be approved by the rights holder.

This is a work of fiction. Unless otherwise indicated, all the names, characters, businesses, places, events and incidents in this book are either the product of the author's imagination or used in a fictitious manner.

Front cover design by Cody Sexton.
(Anxiety Press)

ISBN: 9781068626104

Also by James Jenkins

Sun Bleached Scarecrows
The Swine, The Pig and The Porker
Life in Dirt (Short Stories)

FOR JOEY AND RENDY

BLUE TIGER

Dicky Farrell was a ruthless piece of shit. Anyone misfortunate enough to make his acquaintance would confirm this. Now, 'shit' is a strong word, even given its overuse, and therefore popularity, with anyone who has such a potty mouth. But a shit he most certainly was. His brief existence of but two years in the city of Bristol had been one of misery. Whoever crossed him, stood in his way, ended up suffering, discarding souls on his way up the ladder of the city's criminal underworld, blinking over their demise disregard-less. At the beginning he had wondered if it would even be possible to obtain these goals using his usual means, but Dicky had learnt to evolve. Evolve probably wasn't entirely accurate. Dicky Farrell not being the man he now was. It was a world where his true persona could thrive. Because of such success that Dicky'd now found himself in, a position that only the most dedicated lowlifes could hope to be in, and in such a short period of time too. He believed it was his ruthless ability to "get shit done" as he called it, regardless of the impact it would have elsewhere. Coupled with a total lack of moral compass he'd elevated in good favour with his notoriously cruel and unpredictable Boss. Such an asset was invaluable to a man like Bobby Cavendish, a man whose own reputation was far short of a nursery teacher.

Unlike Dicky, Bobby was a charming man. Some would even call him a gentleman. A stranger in the street would say nothing bad about him, should they chance a random encounter with this deceivingly evil man. If, of course, you hadn't crossed him. Indeed, some people may not be aware of the reputation that followed Bobby Cavendish or the stories. The stuff of urban legends. Stories, how Bobby was known to cause serious injury, perhaps death (depending on the mood that took his fancy) with the most unlikely of objects. Bobby excelled in simple weapons: pain designed hardware for drawn out agony. Many people would think a toilet brush a basic household item commonly used for cleaning excrement from the toilet bowl, an unlikely weapon. Bobby Cavendish however, had an imagination that would make the most twisted minds cringe. Even Dicky admitted that Bobby could go too far, though he cared not for the persons unfortunate to be on the receiving end of such treatment. Perhaps this was one of the reasons that Farrell (who rarely feared anyone) was very keen to impress his psychotic boss.

BACK TO BASICS

18 Months earlier…

The sleek black Mercedes – Bobby Cavendish's chariot – prowled up the badly pot-holed entry road. An isolated industrial brick building with metal shutters awaited Cavendish ahead. One of the roller doors opened halfway and as the Merc parked close, a man in his mid-thirties ducked out from under the opening. The well-suited individual had an air of authority about him Bobby observed whilst his hired muscle opened the car door.

"Mr Cavendish, it's a pleasure to meet you. I offer my deepest apologies for the circumstances." The respectful and genuine greeting pleased Bobby. It was so hard to find good manners these days. Too many of these young wannabes had in Bobby's humble opinion, a misplaced belief that politeness was a weakness. Only a couple of weeks ago he'd had to cut the hand off a youth who had offered a fist in reply to Bobby's outstretched hand. The lad had perhaps been unfortunate to catch Bobby Cavendish on a uniquely stressful day. 'I don't see what you're crying about!' he had said to the inconsolable teen clutching the bloody stump. 'At least now you have an excuse for refusing to shake your elder's hand.' The man awaiting him now clearly had a better grasp of basic common decency. Bobby wondered if the man in front of him realised the impact his manners were having. There were other places Bobby would have liked to be on a cold autumn Sunday morning, than a deprived and desolate industrial estate on the outskirts of Bristol. The unit that he found himself at today belonged to an associate of Bobby's, Tyson Boswell. He and Boswell had enjoyed a long-standing professional relationship. Boswell's incredible influence throughout the traveller community had proven to be invaluable to Bobby Cavendish countless amounts of time in his own line of work. Boswell was also one of Bobby's best customers when it came to shifting thousands of pounds worth of narcotics. It was this special relationship that afforded the level of sympathy Boswell was being allowed today. A very large amount of cocaine moving from Cavendish to Boswell had been confiscated whilst in transit by a police sting. The man who had been driving the transit van on behalf of Tyson Boswell had been the obvious fall guy. The police had placed the man under arrest and nobody on the outside held much hope of him being released any time soon. Boswell assured Bobby that the lad was from good stock and would keep his trap shut, but theories on another rat within Boswell's ranks had been investigated. So, Bobby found himself today ready to administer furious vengeance to the accused.

Turning over the man as well as half the cost of the confiscated narcotics had been agreed between Bobby and Boswell. Ordinarily, Bobby would have preferred to reclaim his entire fee AND have the rat but sometimes a compromise was the best option. If Bobby Cavendish had learnt one thing about travellers (other than not calling them *Pikeys*), then it was to not fuck with them. Privately he conceded that it was perhaps best for both men's professional and physical future that Boswell had sent one of his soldiers instead. Judging by first impressions, Bobby was pleased that at least the traveller had gotten that right.

He walked directly up to Boswell's man who now offered his hand to Bobby, another mark in his good books. The two henchmen accompanying him moved between the men in practiced defence of their boss. "Play nice boys. This one's got manners." The two big men backed off as Bobby took the offered hand.

"Dicky Farrell," said the man attached to the firm handshake.

"Apologies from the boss he couldn't be here today, but hopefully I can assist you with anything you need Mr Cavendish."

Bobby liked this Farrell indeed. Strong handshake, polite and seemingly eager to please. Yes. All the boxes were being ticked!

"Good to meet you Dicky. Apologies accepted, it's nice to see Tyson has improved his personnel recruitment. I like a man with manners. Formalities aside, what have you got for me Mr Farrell?"

"Connor Tierney. Overzealous little prick who had a misplaced vision of getting rich quick I'm afraid. We have a couple reliable sources claiming he had been selling information to the police. Coupled with the sums of cash we found in his house – we're confident the rat has been sniffed out. He won't admit it yet, but I didn't want to make too much of a start without you Sir."

Sir! Yes, yes, yes! Bobby really was growing fond of this Dicky Farrell. "That's very considerate of you Dicky. Can I call you Dicky or would you prefer Mr Farrell? I'd be personally honoured if you called me Bobby. After all, we're all friends here."

"Dicky is fine with me Mr Cav... Bobby," Dicky corrected himself from his intentional mistake as the two men shook hands again.

"Shall we get started Dicky?" Cavendish asked as Dicky politely ushered for him to follow into the building under the shutters. "Lionel, bring the tool kit. We might need it. Joe, my apron too. Things could get messy," he ordered the two muscle men.

Bobby Cavendish looked at the unconscious naked form of a man tied to the wooden chair. Dicky hadn't been kidding, there was barely a mark on the bound and gagged individual. Bobby scanned the interior of the building. The industrial unit had clearly been a commercial mechanic's work room. There were still some odd tools laying around but nothing that inspired him. He leaned his head back searching for the right instrument, a corrugated asbestos roof loomed over their heads. A killer in its own right but waiting a couple of decades for the man to possibly die of lung cancer was even too drawn out for Bobby. He had to admit that his usual creativity when it came to inducing pain and torture just wasn't there today. That's when he came up with another idea.

"Dicky, how would you feel about taking the reins for me on this one?"

"Bobby I'm honoured. Although I must admit I'm not sure if I will be able to live up to your own legendary reputation." Dicky, like anyone who had spent so much as an hour in Bristol's underworld had heard of the stories that cemented Bobby Cavendish's reputation.

"Nonsense! Dicky, I have full faith in you. What have you got?"

Dicky looked around quickly searching for something to impress the hardened gangster, his eyes settled on a crowbar that had been disregarded by the previous occupier of the garage. Hardly original he mused slightly worried that the great Mr Cavendish wouldn't approve. Bobby followed his gaze.

"Yes Dicky! That will do. Sometimes the oldies are the best. That's what I always say isn't it boys?" Bobby laughed looking at the two henchmen.

"Yes boss," the two men replied together.

"Back to basics Mr Farrell. I like it very much." Bobby did like it very much, very much indeed. This Dicky character was growing on him more by the minute. How the hell an uneducated tosser like Boswell, ended up with such a fine stead as this was a wonder to Cavendish.

"Shall I try to wake up the lazy irk Bobby Sir?"

"Oh yes Dicky that would be most pleasing. Maybe a shattered kneecap would rouse him from his slumber." Bobby rubbed his hands in glee.

If Dicky had any reservations about administering severe violence on the man in the chair, then he hid it well as he swung the metal bar at full arc into the unconscious victim's left knee cap. A resounding crack and pop exploded from the startled body as the man came screaming back into consciousness. Bobby couldn't help but smile. Had Dicky used the blunt side of the crowbar intentionally he wondered? That's what he would have done, blunt force trauma to get the blood flowing. The pointed edge would be saved for a later blow now the man was fully awake.

"Are you with us Connor?" Dicky calmly asked the man screaming through the gag. There was no coherent reply from the dribbling mess, Bobby watched with pensive excitement. Dicky sensed that his next move would be crucial in Bobby's assessment of him, so he swung the crowbar again this time using the pointed claw like end to shatter and imbed itself into Connor's right kneecap. The blood curdling crunch of bone and cartilage entwined with the man's screams of agony filled the garage interior as full as it did Bobby Cavendish's beating heart. Oh yes! I really do like this Dicky! Bobby was feeling an overwhelming sense of pride over the lad. It's exactly the way he would have done it when he had been a younger, less creative, enforcer. That was okay, Dicky could learn, Bobby would be only too happy to be his teacher. His thoughts were interrupted as the man with shattered legs passed out from the pain. This wasn't a problem to Bobby. He had seen enough. The lad had probably done it and Boswell had given his word that this was the rat. Good enough for me, Bobby shrugged to himself.

"Finish this slippery bugger off for me Lionel. Clean up after yourself, Joe will help," Bobby gestured to the big men.

"Dicky. You have been most helpful. Please accept my deepest gratitude to you and your boss. I look forward to seeing you again, I'll be passing my compliments to Mr Boswell myself on your professionalism." Bobby shook the younger man's hand again.

"Thank you, Bobby. It has been an absolute pleasure to work alongside you. I hope we meet again under better circumstances."

"I have a distinct feeling that we will indeed Mr Farrell. Don't worry about all this mess here, my boys will take care of everything. Until we meet again."

Dicky left the garage waiting until he was firmly out of sight before expelling the acidic contents of his guts.
Cavendish's bodyguards had already been choosing hand tools from the bag as he shook the gangster's hand. He could hear the damage they were making to the man's skull as he exited the building. It had been these sounds that tipped Dicky's usually strong stomach over the edge. It would all be worth it though if as he suspected it all went to plan. It had been a lucky escape in hindsight, Connor wasn't guilty of ratting on anybody. The only thing the unfortunate lad had been guilty of was being in the wrong place at the wrong time. If Connor had talked it would have been to protest innocence, but then so would a rat if he had Bobby Cavendish standing in front of him. Nobody was going to find the rat, Dicky knew this. Connor just made a good fall guy, Boswell was only too happy to give someone, anyone to Cavendish just to keep the peace. Dicky had been waiting for this opportunity for some time and now he was finally in good favour with the great man himself. If all followed to plan, then Dicky would also be rid of working for Tyson Boswell.

The black Mercedes pulled away from the industrial unit with Bobby Cavendish in the large and luxurious back seats. He waited as the ringing tone sounded in his ear. He was like a kid on Christmas eve. Full of anxious excitement. He knew he could have what he wanted but protocol must be followed. Permission would need to be granted.
Finally, the phone on the other side picked up. "Hello Mr Cavendish," a thick Irish accent belonging to Tyson Boswell

answered. "Hello Tyson. You've got something I want. You can consider your final balance paid. Dicky Farrell will be working for me from now on."

***

Back in current time, Dicky was enjoying some down-time in his favourite haunt: Bobby Cavendish's very exclusive Blue Tiger, strip club. It was without a shadow of doubt *the* best strip club that Dicky had ever thought himself lucky enough to grace. The girls were very hot, young too. Not illegal young but close. There was heavy emphasis on the girls to offer and charge for extra services and though not mandatory, those who refused rarely lasted long. There was one who had been made an exception of. She had only been expected to serve drinks and welcome customers. Dicky knew most of the girls incredibly well (in and out), but *this* beautiful creature was thus unspoiled. The somewhat uncommon and violent threat had been given to Cavendish's employees that it remains this way. Unfortunately for Dicky, this just made her even more desirable to him and he had every intention of defying Cavendish's wishes. Dicky knew he had a chance with the girl and that was all he needed to make up his mind. Money can make men do the stupidest things but to Dicky, pussy was much more powerful, and he had to have *this* one.

One of the well-used vaginas in the club danced provocatively, inches from his face. The girl to whom it belonged followed his gaze. He suddenly became distracted. Dicky was staring at the forbidden girl who had just walked out from behind the bar with a tray of Corona bottles, a lemon slice in each.

Parochial Pigs

"You bored of my pussy Dicky?" she asked with mock offence. Dicky ignored her and continued to stare at the girl setting the tray of drinks down in front of some rowdy suited businessmen. Men in poorly fitted suits and overbearing guts that swelled over their waistlines.

"Emily's off-limits Dicky, you know that. How 'bout you and me go out back? I know you love it when I do that thing to your dick."

Dicky's semi erect penis had lost all its blood flow now. The girl above wasn't unattractive to him, her fake tits, orange glow and auburn hair. Ordinarily this would have been his type, in fact she had been his type many times before but something about this Emily's natural beauty evoked something in Dicky. She was nothing like the other girls and did they not say that variety was the spice of life?

"You can fuck off now Dee," he said standing up from the chair.

Without giving the girl's face another glance, he tossed a five-pound note on the table and headed towards Emily.

"You fucking wanker! A fiver?" she called out to the back of his now distant head.

***

Dicky knew Emily would be coming off shift in a minute. Off record, Dicky had taken Emily out for a couple drinks over the last week, he could be a proper Romeo when he wanted to. The girl had been putty in his hands, but she wanted to take things slow. He, of course, had played along, promising her that she was the one. It had been a close call tonight. If she had seen him with Dee, it could have fucked up all his

'hard' work. As far as he knew she was meant to be working the door tonight, one of the favoured jobs that Cavendish allowed the girl.
Luckily, she hadn't seen him. He followed her into the changing rooms and came up behind her. He put his hands over her eyes gently, making the young girl jump and spin round in surprise.

"Dicky!" she yelped with a huge smile on her face.

"Hello sweetheart, still on for tonight?" he whispered in her ear.

"Yeah, give me half hour, see you at mine yeah?"

Dicky winked and left Emily to get herself changed. He knew Cavendish wasn't about tonight, but it wouldn't do if tongues started flapping on them leaving the club together. After tonight though, he wouldn't need to worry about all the sneaking around anymore. He'd won her trust and she had invited him over to hers. Dicky knew that meant one thing. Tomorrow she'd be another notch on the bed post (or rather, the coat hook.) It was too risky to keep fucking her after that, being as this was the sort of girl that only let you in if there was a future, and Dicky Farrell had no intention of being a one pussy man.

He left the club through the back, exiting onto a quiet service road. One of the dancers that hadn't quite yet taken Dicky's fancy, was having a fag break out of the club. The girl's name he couldn't remember, and he was too busy smirking at the older lady she was talking to. The older woman looked like her entire wardrobe came from an eighties jumble sale mixing a red floral ankle length dress with a winter puffer jacket. Dicky wasn't buying that wig for one second either. The "crazies" had certainly been about lately. Trying to talk to the girls about their sins and join their church. The sort of thing he considered mad-bull-shit. He gave the girl a wink as he walked by and blanked the other woman, not wanting to waste his time. After-all, Dicky had a big date tonight.

BOBBY CAVENDISH, THE MAN, THE LEGEND

With the last tent peg expended, Bobby Cavendish threw the rubber mallet to the ground. Fatigued, he rubbed his aching right arm.

"Get rid of this," he motioned to the dying bloody mass strapped to the chair.

The two colossal bodybuilders nodded their bald heads in unison towards their boss. Programmed androids, they both set about dealing with the mutilation. Cavendish hadn't got much from the girl before she gave up, not that he was convinced she knew any more than he already did. After the fifth or sixth tent peg had gone in, he had decided it was best for her to be retired. It hadn't all been for nothing, the journalist story did interest him. Around about the third peg, Chantelle had divulged to him that she had taken money from the woman for information about his girls. Apparently, she had been keen to find *one* girl in particular.

Bobby Cavendish considered himself a gentleman. Perhaps in his own logic he was. He treated all *his* girls well, allowing them to choose when and if they wanted the extra cash. Providing, they paid his commission. After all, ground rent wasn't cheap these days. All he asked in exchange for the reliable supply of custom and rigorous security he provided was complete transparency. Bobby found that one way of making sure these girls maintained complete loyalty to him was to offer them a reliable and steady supply of drugs. This was a highly efficient method and particularly beneficial as he controlled the drug distribution throughout most of the area.

He had always liked Chantelle; she was one of his favourites. The drug abuse had started to erode the girl's once flawless features. He'd known that sooner or later she had to go. Not that she would have known this herself. It just made her recent deceit even more puzzling. Why risk everything she had for just a couple of hundred extra pounds? Whoever this prying so-called journalist was, Bobby was sure it was no coincidence that three of his dealers had been caught out by police drug raids. Fortunately for Bobby, his hands were in many pies, including that of the local police force. So far, the arrested men had kept their mouths shut, being very good for their long-term health. But it was the girl the journalist was interested in that worried Bobby the most, he wasn't prepared to share her with anyone else. Turning his mind back to the current issue of now being one "dancer" short, he allowed the constant distraction of the new girl, Emily, to return to the forefront of his thoughts. Bobby had liked her from the off, pure innocence. She was different from his usual girls, natural titties but still full and that little itty-bitty waist of hers helped emphasise their size. The girl had an innocent face with full lips that promised to suck a cricket ball through a hose pipe. Bobby hadn't decided what to do with her yet. The petite brunette had been brought to his attention from a small-time dealer he had on his books: The little prick had been bragging about one of his customers and how he was working on getting into her panties. The girl had missed payment on her tick a couple of times, and he was hoping to use this as a means to "get his willy wet." Bobby'd sent one of his boys – Dicky Farrell – to meet the girl and told the small fry dealer to wipe her dept, which it turned out was very small and only for a bit of weed. The girl accepted a job at the club. Happy to take the employment waiting tables and the occasional dance on the podium if she wanted it. He'd been charmed by the girl: far more cultured than his usual calibre of employee. She had been firm but polite, requesting not to dance one on one for the customers. Emily had also made it clear that she had no current desire to wear anything less than the albeit still-revealing slit dress (of which was standard for the girls to wear before private dances). Of course, Bobby had agreed.

Bobby had dealt with his fair share of aggrieved dads and overzealous protective brothers. It paid to give these girls time to settle first and there was also the small problem of her lack of desire for hard drugs. Normally this would have been problematic for Bobby but there was indeed something special about her. She was fiercely dedicated to her job already and in this business the niceties from the girls to the male punters was just so fake. The more experienced girls were getting through their shift to pay for the next big high and though Emily hadn't yet been subjected to this grittier line of work, her attitude was nevertheless refreshing. She genuinely seemed to show a true happiness in everything she did. Bobby found himself captivated by her, eagerly waiting for Emily to arrive on shift so he could watch her go about her business from the CCTV monitor in his private office. Something very rare was happening inside Bobby Cavendish, something he had only ever once before experienced. Bobby Cavendish was in love.

CLEAN LIVING

Bobby fed the ripe cream covered strawberry into her delicious mouth. Cream ran down her perfectly formed chin. But that didn't matter, he used his finger to wipe it away before lapping it up as Emily laughed again in that way that made him full of love. Bobby leaned in for a kiss and she willingly gave it. The kiss became a passionate embrace, their lips pressing into one another as hands ran wild. Bobby laid down on top of her pushing the contents of the picnic hamper aside. It didn't matter if anyone was watching, this was his moment and he was in control of it. His hands found her round breasts as her nipples hardened under her white vest… No. No. She was wearing a beautiful summer frock… Yes! It was yellow too, he decided. He pushed himself into her pelvis and reached down to pull up the hem of her summer slip. Sliding his hand up towards…

Knock Knock

"For fucks sake!" fumed Bobby, pulling his hand out of his trousers. He was just getting to the good part: *Later my darling*, he said to the Emily of his imagination.

"Come in…" The office desk hid his modesty as Dicky walked through the door.

"Ah! Dicky my boy. Take a seat," so gestured – Ordinarily, he would make his visitors stand but Dicky: This lad was alright.

"Thanks Boss," Dicky said as he took up the offer and settled into the vacant chair.

"How can I help?"

"I'm afraid I don't come with good news boss."

"Dicky, you know you can call me Bobby. You're not the same as the rest of these parasites round here, you've got manners, Dicky."

"Thanks… Bobby." The pride evident on Dicky's face. "So, enlighten me."

"Like I said, Bobby. It's not good news. Do you remember Mark Ross?"

"Mark Ross? Yes, the health and safety officer. The little jobsworth who tried to close down my building site?"

"That's the one."

"Well what about him? He's been buried under several thousand tons of concrete for the past few months. We should know Dicky!" Bobby couldn't contain a little chuckle as he replayed Mark Ross' last hours alive. "That was one of our first jobs together."

HEALTH & SAFETY GONE MAD

Nine months earlier…

The Mercedes pulled up to the building site entrance, fighting its way through the waiting crowd of construction workers stationed in the car park. The chain link was wrapped tightly and preventing Bobby's car access to the site.

"Why aren't they working Lionel?" Bobby asked, "Get out and see if you can find the site manager amongst these primitive beasts."

Lionel stepped his huge bulk out. The suspension sprung back, seemingly relieved, rid of this giant man. Bobby gazed as the workers naturally gave the former strongman space. Eventually, a man wearing a shirt and tie emerged clasping a clipboard.

"That's him." Bobby waited for Joe, his other bodyguard to open the passenger door for him to step out. Bobby turned his attention straight to the site manager, looking him up and down in disgust. His physique gave him away, swelling gut, flabby arms, the man didn't look like he'd done a second of manual labour in his life. That was the problem with these educated types. Straight to the top without learning the business first. It was little wonder that this particular pen pusher had failed to keep the site open.

"Why is my site closed?" he snapped.

"Sorry, sir. But who are you?" the site manager enquired with a professional air, lost on Bobby.

"Who am I?! Who the fuck *are* you?!"

Lionel stepped in front of his boss, towering down upon the little man in the shirt and tie. "You don't ask Mr Cavendish questions. Mr Cavendish asks you." The terrified look on the site manager's face was evident for everyone to see. Bobby guessed by the looks of amusement from the rest of the workers that the site manager in front of him was not a popular figure. That's okay, he could work with it.

"Oh… Mr Cavendish! Please accept my humblest apologies. I haven't had the pleasure. My names Roger Smy and I am the senior site manager." He extended a hand towards Bobby, quickly swatted away by Joe. Roger Smy recoiled. Joe's hands were like a couple of meat mallets.

"Don't touch Mr Cavendish," Joe affirmed – delicately, slowly.

"Why is my fucking site closed? I will not ask you again," Bobby demanded, playing up to the attentive crowd.

"It's not my fault sir, I tried to keep them away, yet they insisted on closing the site until we could meet their standards for dust suppression. See, most of the new workers haven't been face fitted for their FFP3 disposable masks."

Bobby pulled the mock look of confusion, turning to the crowd who were gathering for the 'Bobby Cavendish' show. "Can someone tell me what the *fuck, this*, snivelling little toad in front of me, is saying?"

A worker moved to the front of the foray – a big man with a bustling beard, tattoo's – now this man looks like he could run a building site.

"Hello, Mr Cavendish, sir. I believe I know what 'Smee' is trying to say, HSE aren't happy with the dust masks and they want us to buy an extractor for the dust when we're cutting."

Manners! Bobby hadn't expected to encounter many on this particular building site, this man had proved him pleasantly wrong. He'd have to find out more about him. A promotion could be on the cards.

Roger Smy tried to interrupt, "It's *Smy,* thank you Simon."

"Shut your pencil sucking trap! Simon and I are *trying* to have a conversation here, *man-to-man.*" Bobby took great satisfaction at the jeers coming from the waiting crowd. He'd been right about this Smy from the get-go. These men were not his friends. Roger Smy looked down at the ground.

"Where is this Health and Safety twat now?"

Smy looked up again and opened his mouth to respond but thought better of it, as Bobby glared at him and turned to the other workman.

"Simon. If you would be so kind."

"My pleasure, Mr Cavendish. He's still in the site, Smy here let him stay to check all and anything else he could find."

"What?! He's in my fucking building site and we're all out here scratching our nut sacks! Speak up 'Smee', why have you allowed this to happen!" Bobby enjoyed the worker's smiles as he used Roger Smy's unfortunate moniker. He enjoyed the man's frantic babbling more and more as he tried to defend his actions.

"But they are HSE! We don't have a choice!" Smy stammered.

"Shut the fuck up and open the gates. Lionel, Joe, on me." The three men moved towards the entrance. "And give Dicky a call, I want him on this one."

Roger Smy stepped reluctantly to the locked gate and removed his unwinding tangled mala bead chain of keys. As he fumbled with the padlock, Roger appeared to have a second wind, intending to carry out his job. "Mr Cavendish, please. Mark Ross, the HSE officer, he made it very clear that *nobody* was to *enter* the *site* until *his* inspection was finished."

"Does Mr Cavendish look like *nobody* to you?" Lionel scored and instantly stepped toward the man to grab the keys from his hand.

"Please Mr Cavendish, I can't let you in until he's finished. It's my job on the line!"

"Your job on the line? It is me who decides whether you have a job or not, Mr Smy. You belong to me! Every part of you belongs to me Mr Smy… Joe, take his bollocks off. Let's see who you listen to then."

Lionel held the terrified man, pinning his arms behind his back.

Parochial Pigs

The knife appeared in Joe's hand, and Smy shook in horror.

Even some of the workers who had previously laughed at their boss' treatment backed up, gasping, Bobby, he noticed the change in mood, sensing his audience. It wouldn't do to back out now. Afterall, he had a <u>reputation</u> to keep. Fortunately for Bobby (and perhaps more so for Roger Smy), Simon, the worker who had gone up in Bobby's estimations, let out a laugh, "Look, he's pissed himself!"

The rest of the men joined into a chorus of laughter as the wet patch spread down the site manager's trouser leg. 'AHA! That'll do!' It was probably for the best. Despite the obvious disgust the men shared for their foreman, Bobby still had reservations about cutting men's genitals off in front of so many witnesses. Broken, Roger Smy dropped the keys to the floor slumping to the ground in tears. Simon, picked them up and headed towards the gate, stepping over the snivelling mess on the ground.

He opened the padlock unravelling the heavy chain before turning to Bobby with a smile, "After you, Mr Cavendish."

Bobby stepped through the open gate, stopping beside Simon. "I believe we need to have a talk about promotion. Wait here for me. And somebody, get that soaking-puddle-of-piss out-of-here."

***

Dicky begrudgingly made his way through the rush hour traffic. He'd been tempted to blow out the meet-up that had teared him away from the planned morning of hard sex and even harder drugs. The girl would wait though, they always did. The matter at hand wasn't something he could put off anymore. Unlike the wanton girl he'd left in bed, Doris wouldn't wait. He owed to it her he supposed, and his job was impossible without her help – for now at least. He made a turn onto Folly Lane, heading towards the waste recycling centre when his phone started ringing. The display indicated that it was one of Cavendish's thugs, a call he couldn't ignore.

Dicky answered the phone and pulled over to the side of the road.

"The boss needs you now," came the monotone voice of either Joe or Lionel. Dicky struggled to differentiate between the two big men in person, let alone on the phone. "Come to the building site." The line went dead.

It was the perfect excuse to skip his planned meeting, everyone knew Cavendish came first. Even Doris knew that. He opened the glove box and retrieved another phone and typed out a text before pressing send. It pleased him immensely to know that Bobby Cavendish had called upon him again. The boss had been asking for his assistance more frequently and Dicky was only too happy to oblige. He spun the car around and backtracked the way he'd come.

Dicky navigated his way through the horde of workers up to the site entrance, earning himself more than a few dirty looks. He returned the stares, commanding respect from the onlookers. After exiting the car, he walked to the open gates. His attention was momentarily drawn towards a small fat man who looked like he had been crying and had a wet trouser leg. Dicky deduced that the individual had already met Bobby. Another man, an obvious worker with a cocksure grin greeted

Dicky, "Hello mate, you must be Dicky. Mr Cavendish said to go right in." Apparently, Bobby hadn't upset everyone. He nodded to the man and headed through the gates.

Dicky spotted Bobby standing by a stationary excavator. The machine towered over Bobby and his entourage, even making Joe and Lionel look small in comparison. The three men were talking to another man. Dicky had worked for Bobby long enough to recognise that the man in a white shirt, perfectly ironed trousers and hi-vis jacket was not in his boss' favour.

"Aha! Dicky my boy. Glad you could join us. Let me introduce you to our friend here, Mark Ross. He's from HSE. Actually, he was just about to leave so the building site can reopen," the sarcasm oozed from Bobby.

"No, that is not what is happening here Mr Cavendish. As I have told you already. The site will be closed until further notice and failure to comply will result in an even larger fine and/or a criminal conviction," Mark Ross replied with authority.

Dicky had to admit he was impressed by Ross' confidence. Clearly, he had little or no knowledge about who he was dealing with. But then Dicky wondered if Bobby knew who he was dealing with too. HSE wasn't some rival crime syndicate to be meddled with. This was serious. Unless Mark Ross was inclined to a bribe, then Bobby might have to play ball this time. Something that Dicky knew was highly unlikely. Not for the first time in his tenure under Bobby Cavendish, Dicky was beginning to doubt his boss' judgement. This could put everything at risk. He decided to step in, "Bobby, perhaps Mr Ross would like to take some time to consider this." Turning his attention to the inspector, he added, "I hear that the Bahamas is beautiful this time of year." Mark Ross rolled his eyes and shook his head in disgust, so Dicky pushed on, "What car are you driving Mr Ross? Fancy an upgrade? If not, how about that extension your Mrs is always nagging you about?"

"My employers pay me a generous salary thank you very much, and as for my "Mrs", I have been in an openly gay relationship for several years," Ross said, as Lionel spat on the floor in disgust. "Your boss here has already tried and failed at bribing me. I'm not going to change my mind just because one of his Pitbulls asks me."

Dicky really wished he hadn't said that, if he didn't react to the man's remark then he would appear weak. Unfortunately, Mark Ross had left him no choice.

***

Bobby watched with mixed amusement as Dicky and the inspector conversed. Ordinarily, he wouldn't appreciate one of his minions stepping in over his head, but Dicky was different from the rest. He knew he could trust the younger man's quick thinking. That's why he liked having him around. If it was Joe or Lionel, then Mark Ross would be laying on the ground with a broken skull by now. That could still happen, especially after the last remark that came out of the inspectors' mouth. Bobby watched Dicky's reaction; he was impressed by the lack of emotion his favourite employee's face showed. If Dicky was offended by the slight, then he wasn't giving anything away as he smirked back at Ross. After a moment that could have lasted for eternity but was closer to a split second, Ross reached for his pocket and produced a mobile phone. Bobby was hoping he would do something like that. Now he could see his little 'Pitbull' in action.

***

Dicky searched deep inside of himself for the ability to restrain his emotions. He didn't like being insulted at the best of times, but in front of Cavendish! He deliberated what should be his next move, hoping that Joe or Lionel would make the decision for him when Ross pulled out a phone. No. That wouldn't do. Dicky stepped forward on impulse and head-butted the man, Ross' nose exploded like a volcano. Dropping his phone to the floor he clutched at the broken nose, claret pouring through his fingers.

"What?! I'm... calling... the police," Ross cried out between shuddering breaths.

"Joe, close the gates. Make sure nobody comes in," Bobby ordered.

"My... *sniff* nose! ...*cough* ...he's broken it!"

Dicky turned to Bobby, "What we going to do with him Bobby? He can't leave, not now."

"I... I need to go to hospital..." Blood dribbled from Ross' chin as he tried to stem the bleeding.

"You're not going anywhere sunshine," Bobby said, rubbing his hands together in glee. "For starters, you owe my friend Dicky here an apology."

It was done now, there would be no backing out of this one. Why, oh, why did Bobby have to start something with this bloke. Dicky would rather take his chances with a copper than this Mark Ross. There would be repercussions from this, Dicky was sure. Oh well, this would be on Bobby Cavendish either way. He'd noticed Bobby getting sloppier lately, the man's ego was swelling at an alarming rate. But if Dicky played his cards right – and he fully intended to – then he might be best placed to fill the infamous Cavendish's boots. But he was getting ahead of himself, for now, it was back to the matter at hand.

"What do you want to do with him Bobby?" Dicky pushed.

"What do I want to do with him? What do we want to do with him Dicky? The building site is our playground." Bobby turned around on the spot, hands behind his back looking for some *inspiration*.

"Know how to operate one of those, Dicky?" His eyes had fixed onto the gigantic excavator and its attachment, a massive digging grabber which was designed for biting huge amounts of soil from the ground. The two buckets were like a dinosaur's jaws, only bigger and far from extinct.

Dicky looked up towards the cab of the construction vehicle, he'd had some experience with similar machines, just not on this scale. They couldn't be that different, could they? 'Only one way to find out,' and with that he began to scale the machine.

Mark Ross was beginning to regain some of his senses, the chatter around was quite sobering. Especially when it was his life being decided. Ross wiped away the tears from his eyes and blood from his snout and started to stumble towards the exit. Bobby dragged his attention from the climbing Dicky and focused it back onto the dazed escapee.

Parochial Pigs

"Lionel… bring our friend Mr Ross back, would you?" The big henchman had amazing agility for such a dense looking unit, darting after Ross in an instant and dragging him back to Bobby. "Hit him again for me please Lionel and break his fucking leg while you're at it. We don't want him strolling off again before Dicky works out how to operate that thing."

The crunch of bone was audible even to Dicky, currently sitting nine foot up in the digger's cab. Why couldn't this Mark fucking Ross just take the bloody bribe?! Dicky had no love for the man, but this guy was an honest Joe. People like this didn't deserve to be a victim of organised crime. They represented another world entirely, people that should not be on the receiving end of Bobby Cavendish. Not only that, but this man would also have family and loved ones, who would certainly want answers. Inevitably, the HSE would turn over to the police Ross' last known whereabouts. It wouldn't take them long to interview all the workers and Dicky didn't fancy the humiliated man he'd seen at the front gate keeping his mouth shut. But that was Bobby's problem.

Bobby shouted up to the cab as Dicky leaned out to hear, "He's not going anywhere, see if you can grab him up."

Dicky grabbed the controls of the digger having already familiarised himself with them. The arm swung down in an arc, as the bucket opened like a claw.

"How good are you with that thing? I don't want you to kill him. Not yet anyway, that'll all come later," Bobby chuckled. He was having a very good time. He knew from the off that Dicky had something special. Bobby felt that he'd found a true prodigy in him and took a newfound pleasure in his role as tutor. "Grab him by his neck if you can... but be gentle."

The screams of agony questioned Dicky's already uncalibrated moral compass as the descending excavator inched towards the pleading safety inspector. He didn't know how he would be able to handle the man's torture once he'd reached him with the bucket. He'd administered worse before, but this man was innocent.

"That's it Dicky! Keep it coming," Bobby shouted over to Joe, who was standing twenty feet away by the gates. "See Joe, I told you this Dicky had something special, didn't I?"

"YES BOSS!" shouted joe over the noise of the machine and Ross' screams which had amplified as the bucket drew ever closer.

Dicky couldn't but feel an exalted sense of pride – he really was very vain. Well, if it's between him or me. He pushed the control stick with more urgency and reached the man on the floor. Being as tentative as was possible for an inexperienced operator, Dicky attempted to pick Mark Ross up by his neck using the two serrated buckets as a pincer. Such vehicles are not designed for sensitive operations, as Dicky found out after his attempt.

"You've taken his fucking head off Dicky!" Bobby burst out in laughter, pointing at the decapitated corpse that fell back to the floor. "Never mind. These things don't always work out as planned. It's all trial and error really. Now drop his head out of the bloody scoop thing and get down here." Dicky released Ross' head from the buckets and climbed down from the machine, fighting back his conflicting feelings about the man's death.

"Better luck next time lad." Bobby patted Dicky on the back. "It was still a bloody good show though. Wasn't it boys?"

"Yes boss!" Joe and Lionel chimed.

"You did good today, Dicky. You're a good man."

"Thanks Bobby. Sorry I couldn't get the... the... grabby thing right."

"Ha ha! Take the rest of the day off. You did fine, really. I'll see you at the club later."

Dicky took the dismissal willingly. There would be a lot of heat on this building site now and he was only too happy to put some distance between, him and it. As he walked back towards the gate Bobby called out, "Send that Simon bloke with the tattoos in. I want to lay some concrete."

***

Back in the present time, Dicky watched his boss' glazed eyes return to focus. "Sorry Dicky, I was a million miles away. That was a good one! I bet with some practice you'd of worked that digger out. Anyway, why are we talking about Mark Ross again? The police dropped the investigation, the workers all took a little 'compensation'. My new friend Simon saw to the that. Even that pudgy, little site manager agreed to take a large financial package to fuck off and keep his mouth shut. It can't be the HSE again, the next one they sent had more sense. Now, he knew when to take a bribe. Truth be told, I think I'd have been better off buying the safety equipment after paying everyone off."

"None of those are the problem, Bobby. There was one person... we forgot about." Dicky was tempted to use the word *you*, seeing as Bobby had dug the hole for himself. He couldn't deny he was taking a slice of enjoyment from Bobby's worried face. He wouldn't win any favour by announcing 'I told so', but this was... nice.

"Who the hell is it, Dicky? Why are you keeping me in suspense?"

"It's Ross' partner Bobby. He's been asking a lot of questions to the wrong people. The police are finding it hard to ignore him and that's despite your friends in blue's, influence."

"That's right! I forgot he was one of *them!* So, what's this bloody Nancy boy got his knickers in a twist about? There's plenty more arseholes in the sea. I think we did him a favour myself. Have you talked to this 'boyfriend' yet?" Bobby swallowed uncomfortably, "Christ, it makes you sick just saying it. I've never understood these mincers. The anal passage has one task only Dicky. It's one-way traffic for fucks sake. I don't know, offer him some incentive, money or pain, whatever it takes. You decide, I trust your judgement on this one. The thought of it turns my stomach." Bobby took a sip of his coffee, attempting to wash the image he'd put in his own head away.

"Yes Bobby. Not a problem. I must warn you, I doubt he'll be paid off. I think I've got something in mind though."

"Just get it done Dicky. No come backs on me, okay?"

"You have nothing to worry about Bobby. Consider it done." Dicky got up from the chair, bowing to his boss. The gesture pleased Bobby.

"You keep up all this good work and I'll have to promote you lad. Anyone would think you're after my job!" Bobby laughed in good humour as Dicky left the office. Dicky wasn't laughing, but he turned his back on Bobby, quick to hide the smug grin on his face.
It wasn't just the job he was getting; he was going to get the girl too!

James Jenkins

PANDORA

Her mouth was dry but her pussy wet. She allowed herself to lay back and let the blood flow return to her body as her pulsating clit slowed. She needed more than a few seconds to catch her breath. Her limbs ached from being manipulated but my God she didn't mind, the way he had touched her made up for that. Rolling over to look at him she was disappointed, to say the least, that he had already passed out. She couldn't really blame him. She herself dozed off after some time until waking up alone in her small flat. Emily looked behind her on the empty bed happily remembering the night before. She checked the time on her phone. Four twenty in the morning. He must have worried someone from work would see his car outside, she guessed. At least she would see him at work tomorrow, He'd explain it then.

Emily's attraction to Dicky hadn't been an immediate one. Their first meeting had been one of fear for poor unexpecting Emily. When her dealer, a vile man-child had told her that someone wanted to discuss her small debt she had been absolutely petrified! Even after the little letch had reassured her that she wasn't in trouble she hadn't relished the encounter. Dicky Farrell had turned up to her tiny flat of which she was *still* two hundred pounds overdue on this month. He had seemed friendly enough; explaining that his boss would like to offer her an opportunity to work off the debt and earn some more money on the side. Her initial response to working at a strip club was one of shock and therefore refusal, but as Dicky began to explain she wouldn't actually be gyrating her crotch into men's faces and that her role would be more the nature of a hostess or waitress. It was worth some thought.

Emily hadn't managed to hold down much of a job for a while now. There had been some modelling work to start with, she'd managed to make some decent cash after first moving here, but the last year had been hard. The late nights and the party lifestyle had gained her a few irrefutable contacts but also had lost the more reliable ones. Oversleeping, turning up looking like death, sometimes not turning up at all will do that. She let the cocky well-dressed man now sitting on her fold out sofa bed tell her more about the job opportunity. The thought of buying your weed from your boss certainly had an attractive appeal to it. At least there wouldn't be any drug tests. She agreed to go with Dicky to meet this Bobby Cavendish, her potential employer.
Emily had been charmed by Mr Cavendish. The man had a natural confidence with people, especially women. There had been something else about the man though, she didn't doubt that his friendly and elegant attitude could be quickly replaced with something far more sinister. Emily had to admit the whole idea of working at the strip club and for such a man thrilled her.

After a couple of weeks working at the club, Emily had started to enjoy it. Everything was going great. For the first time in a long while she had money, none of her bills were outstanding. The other girls seemed nice, which was not something she would have first expected. Quite a few of them were into their harder drugs. She guessed this was the reason most of them sold their sex to the persistent punters. Emily didn't judge them for it, they all seemed happy and in control of what they did. She had no intention to follow suit, even for the large sums of money they told her about. But more to her heart, Emily had really become to quite like Dicky. He always singled her out to ask how she was getting on. She didn't have many friends and her previous boyfriends had all been typical stoners with no job prospects. Dicky wore a suit; he was smart, and he was motivated. Emily was only too happy to take him up on his offer for drinks after work one night. That night when they had shared their first drink in a pub some distance away from the club, Dicky had warned her Bobby Cavendish didn't like his staff to have relationships. It was bad for business apparently. Emily didn't mind, it only added to the excitement she felt with Dicky. But that was before last night when she had seen the other side of him.

Emily had almost finished her shift but had seen no sign of Dicky, not wanting to risk any reason for suspicion she didn't ask if anyone had seen him. It was only as she was about to leave that it happened, while wishing a goodnight to the bar staff, a girl she knew and had got on well with called Dee, led a man out from one of the 'private rooms'. Emily knew exactly what the private rooms were for and it was pretty obvious to her at least, that the man coming out of the room had just enjoyed himself very much. She had seen the same look on his face last night in her own bedroom where they had shared something special. The way he had investigated her soul had eroded all her usual apprehension. The soft but strong hands that needed at her naked body tearing away her emotional defences. She had given herself to him completely when all he had wanted was to use her. Holding in the tears that were threatening to burst from her eye sockets, she made for the double doors to the vestibule barely making it to the street outside before the tidal wave of tears erupted.

STICKY DICKY

Dicky was feeling very good about things tonight. Cock sucked by the oh so desperate for it, Dee (he only had to flash a bit of powder these days), he racked himself another line and left the club. Cavendish had a special assignment for him, and Dicky really needed this. He had been craving this sort of trust from Cavendish for a while now and it couldn't have come soon enough for Dicky: A low risk job that would benefit all parties. Diverting any unwanted heat he may find himself in. To let him move further up the ladder. After tonight he would give that bloody 'Doris' a call, give her some of the information she kept nagging him for. They were paying him after all.

All business concluded for the night he thought he would reward himself a visit with his newest conquest. He started his car and James Brown filled his ears from the radio.

"I feeeel good!"

Dicky did feel good and he knew he was good. That girl had lost her shit last night, she'd been wetter than Niagara Falls. To top it off, her eyes told Dicky that she was falling in love with him of which he found hilarious. He now knew that it was this innocence that made him want to tick her off his bucket list. He guessed he could chance maybe one or two more shags with the girl before anyone started noticing. She would be brought down gently of course. Not before he had another go tonight though, he'd see if he could push things a bit further this time. Make it a bit kinky, he teased himself, whilst rubbing his cock under the steering wheel.

Dicky pressed the buzzer at the front of the now familiar flat and waited for the click of the door release. A tinny female voice screeched at him instead.

"You. Fucking. Wanker!" the intercom spat.

"Babe, what's the matter? It's me, Dicky," he pleaded none the wiser to why he was on the receiving end of such a hostile reception.

"I saw you with her Dicky, you're a lying twat! And with Dee for fucks sake!"

Bollocks. He rolled his eyes. Apparently, he hadn't been paying attention to the time today. It wasn't the end of the world; it was bound to happen at some point. Best thing he could do now was calm her down and make sure she kept her mouth shut. Shit, if he played this right then he could be on for some serious make up sex. By the sound of Emily's current mood though that would take some doing.

"Look, babe just let me in, I can explain."

"Yeah right Dicky, I'm not stupid. I know what I saw."

"I know Em. I've fucked up big time, but I owe you an explanation at least. Please let me in."

There were a few seconds delay, he could hear the heartbroken girl's sobs slightly abating now. Finally, the buzz came through the little speaker allowing him into the lobby. Dicky walked into the lift and hit the number for Emily's floor.

James Jenkins

The talk hadn't gone to plan. You could in fact say it had gone completely tits up. The girl had seemed calm enough at first, but that changed quickly when he tried to deny it. It was a fair cop he supposed. She wouldn't settle down again after that. Things just got worse. It was all just a bit too much for Dicky and even more so that the chance of a fuck had already faded. No matter what line he tried to spin, she just got worse, threatening to tell Cavendish all about them. He hadn't liked that, his temper lost, he pushed her into the hallway wall. She flew back easily from Dicky's heavy and unexpected push, her head hitting the plaster board. Ordinarily such a blow could cause a small shock of pain, perhaps the plasterboard may dent. The person would maybe rub their head and carry on, but Emily didn't. Her head just stayed in the place of contact making some small jerking movements. Then he noticed her eyes. They had been filled with fear just before her legs gave way and she fell limp to the floor. That wasn't without taking part of the wall with her and the coat hook that was imbedded into the back of her skull.

The girl was still twitching so he knew she was alive. He couldn't risk taking her to the hospital, that wasn't going to be an option. This was going to cause a shit load of bad news for Dicky if anyone found out. He would have to arrange this carefully.

HE DOES HAVE A HEART

Bobby Cavendish would never have thought it possible to kill anybody by force feeding them a five-hundred-piece puzzle but then as he had learnt many times before, put a gun to somebody's head and they will mostly do anything for you. It wasn't the eating that had killed her, she was struggling to breathe around the time piece eighty- four had gone down her throat. Shame too. She'd gone before her time.

He could tell there was more Dee wasn't telling him but none of that mattered now. It had been two weeks since Emily had last been seen. Days of re-examining the CCTV footage drew a clear picture for Bobby. Did these dick heads think he was that stupid? It had been like watching a better-acted soap opera that had all the bases covered. Sex, lies, tears, he'd watched it all. There wasn't a room, nook, or cranny in the place that didn't have cameras.

The intel he'd extracted from Dee tonight had been very useful, he knew that she sold information on the girl to the journalist. A stone in his shoe for weeks and up until now seemed impossible to find. After his darling Emily had not turned up for work three days in a row, he'd sent his trusted soldier Dicky Farrell to check on her. Perhaps she'd been unwell. He had made sure to remind Dicky to let her know if she needed anything, anything at all, then she shouldn't hesitate to ask. He would have gone there himself, but Bobby wasn't used to these feelings. He'd found himself as nervous as a schoolboy when he tentatively called her mobile –

cancelling the call before it even rang. The anxious excitement that tore his guts apart every time he thought about her was stronger than how he felt about his own brand of recreational violence, of which often seemed his raison d'êtra when sunk within its depths. Even tonight with Dee, something had changed in him. His heart just hadn't been in it. It was a fucking puzzle, for fucks sake! There was no getting around it, his concentration level was all over the place. Normally, if he liked a girl then he would just take her, but Emily was sacred to him. She had pride and he knew that she wasn't the girl that would give it to him immediately, unless he physically took it from her. He had found himself respecting this trait unfortunately for the first time.

No one had seen the girl, Dicky said that her flat was empty. The landlord confirmed that she had sent him the last payment and left. He could only assume that this journalist had found her, perhaps she had gone back to her family. Neither of them had been seen for some time now. He was heartbroken at first. Days spent moping around wondering what if, but then his first bout with normal human feelings had been momentarily interrupted. Firstly, by overhearing some gossip. Rumour had it the girl was spotted running out of the club in tears on the last day she was there. He had confirmed this after watching the camera feedback. This had led to him to investigate what exactly had made her leave in such a dramatic fashion. It was what she had seen that confused him the most. Dee and Dicky coming out of one of his pleasure rooms.

Bobby actively encouraged the girls in his club to seduce the men that worked for him, there was a lot you could find out about a person when they thought they weren't being watched and vulnerable to their desires. Those that worked for him weren't exempt for paying for extra services either, so it was a great investment on his behalf. Freebies were not tolerated, nor was failing to declare commission for using his club to fuck in. Dee hadn't exactly been cutting her smack bill down lately either and that told Bobby she was getting her money from somewhere. She hadn't missed a payment in weeks. He had trusted Dicky though and would, at first, give him the benefit of the doubt, given his great work of late. Bobby decided to have Dee followed. But he hadn't completely let Dicky of the hook yet, so he used one of his other blokes and yes, he had delivered!

He was shocked to hear that the journalist was back, worse still, Dee had apparently spent a full two hours spilling her beans to the woman. Dee hadn't even tried that hard to be discreet about it, opting to meet the older woman with the limp in Bobby's greasy spoon. He had to think about what this meant for him. Emily could still be out there in this city somewhere just waiting for him to sweep her off her feet. The fantasy had swept through his mind a thousand times. How she would react to his overwhelming love and the riches he could offer. He must find this journalist tonight. Now that he had dealt with Dee he had been rewarded. He knew where the journalist was going. One of his formerly trusted members of staff she was meeting had piqued his interest. *This* certain individual had very much been back on his radar of late.

He watched the body language changing between the girl and Dicky through the endless hours of camera footage. Bobby experienced a whirlwind of emotions.

"NO! MEANS! FUCKING! NO!" he shouted at the Dicky on- screen. Bobby had told him she was off limits. His usually relaxed demeanour shattered by a rare outburst of anger. It's a pity, he thought, Dicky Farrell had been on his way to great things. He would have fun with this one. HA! But first, he was going to head to the garden store. He would have to be creative for this and did so hope that the journalist liked cacti.

WET-BLANKET

Things just hadn't been the same since Emily 'died'. Dicky could feel the tension around the club and this business with the journalist hadn't helped much either. Bobby hadn't phoned him once this week, Dicky wasn't worried that her disappearance was linked to him. He knew he was too good for that. Maybe Cavendish was even softer than he let on, Dicky'd certainly noticed the way Bobby had been moping around like a wet blanket. He'd been doing it ever since the girl disappeared. Dicky felt he had just the news to change all that, this would win him back in favour of Cavendish and get his own career back on track.

Mark Ross' widowed partner had not been an accommodating man when Dicky turned up at his suburban detached house, uninvited. He'd threatened to call the police when Dicky confirmed who his employer was. Persistence had been the key to unlocking the door, so to speak. Mr Ross' ex-partner, Keith Barwick, didn't appear to have much on Bobby Cavendish or indeed Dicky himself. What Keith did make firmly clear though was he wasn't going to let it go without a fight. Fortunately for Dicky and perhaps Keith, both men were able to come to an arrangement. As it turned out, when both had laid their cards out on the table, it was discovered they had a way of helping each other out.

Dicky walked through the doors of the Blue Tiger, ordinarily he would be greeted with more than a few friendly smiles, at the very least from the desperate girls dancing on the pole but nobody was returning his greetings today. He supposed it was the cold shoulder after pushing Dee aside. Come to think of it, he hadn't seen her around lately. Imagining her heartbroken over him helped regain some of his usual arrogance. Dicky walked over to one of the newer girls, she was pretty enough he supposed and asked/demanded a dance. The girl looked over to one of the door staff who nodded to her before she turned her back on him. Little bit strange, he'd never had that happen before. Oh well, the girl was new. Maybe she just didn't know him yet? He'd soon change that once they got into the private room.

The dance hadn't gone anything like he'd hoped. Aside from being moody and distant, the girl flat out refused to give him any extras – even after offering her money. She threatened to call the bouncer if he didn't leave it. Dicky didn't like the vibe of the place – it was all out of whack – he'd put that right, once he got his foot in the door of Bobby's office again. The boss hadn't answered his call earlier or returned it, but Dicky knew Bobby would be upstairs.

The girl showed no emotion as he paid her for the unsatisfactory dance and made an exit. He would bring it up with Bobby, can't have these girls refusing to play ball! Dicky walked up the staircase which led to Cavendish's office, Joe and Lionel barred the way, which wasn't hard for them.

"Alright boys? Is the boss about?" Dicky asked casually.

"Boss is busy. Come back tomorrow," one of the bodyguards said. Dicky couldn't tell which.

"Come on lads! Tell him it's me."

"He said to tell you, *Dicky*, come back tomorrow," came the henchman's reply.

"Fine… just tell him that Ross' fella is taken care of. It's done." Dicky wasn't exactly lying.

"Yeah, he knows," said Joe, or maybe Lionel.

What was that all about? Come back tomorrow? And how did Bobby know about Keith?

Dicky left the club defeated. Less than a month ago, he'd been enjoying the red-carpet treatment by Bobby. It was obvious the older man had some weird desire to be a father figure towards him, but now the attention and special treatment had dried up. Something was wrong, maybe he hadn't been as careful as he believed. Surely not! He'd thought of everything, hadn't he? But if Cavendish knew about Keith Barwick and their deal, then that was very worrying indeed. He reasoned that if Bobby *did* know what he and Keith had discussed, he'd already be dead. Instead, he decided not to worry about Bobby Cavendish. If Keith did what he agreed to and with all the information Dicky had given him, then Dicky Farrell was next in line for the throne.

He retrieved the phone from his jacket, the display told him it was Doris calling. Good. That was a good sign, Keith had been true to his word. All he had to do now was give that journalist a bit more info on Cavendish. He'd already arranged to meet her later. Perhaps that throne was coming sooner than he could have planned.

NO LIMITS

Seeing the little bugger in his club was one thing but having to watch that cretin trying to get off with one of his girls too, that was something else. Bobby Cavendish wanted to drag the prick up there right now and administer him some creative pain. He had no doubt that his beloved Emily's disappearance had something to do with this "Dicky - fucking - Farrell". He'd trusted this ungrateful wretch, Bobby genuinely believed he'd found himself a prodigy. But people let you down, he was used to it and there was only one way to move on from that.

He'd been blinded. There was just too much going on at one time and Dicky had just been another person willing to lighten the load of the dirty work. His enlightenment to this feeling of 'love' had mired his usual level-headed thinking. That said, Dicky Farrell was going to die a slow and painful death, regardless of him knowing or not about Emily's whereabouts.

THE GIRL WAS OFF FUCKING LIMITS!

Bobby had watched the camera footage. Sickening. He had to watch all of Dicky Farrell's 'private' videos too. The man was a cockroach. He had none of the gentlemanly decorum that Bobby possessed. It almost made Bobby feel sorry for Dee, the way Dicky had discarded her. He himself had taken quite a liking to Dee when she'd first joined the club (not like how he felt for Emily, that was another level), but it wasn't to be. Obviously, Bobby had "sampled the fruits", but he just didn't know how to talk to girls on a personal level. He could tell she was only doing it to please him because of who he was. He didn't hold it against her. But Dicky! That parasite knew how to make them putty in his hands. Bobby thought it was absurdly unfair. It was true what they said – nice guys finish last.

He watched Dicky through the CCTV monitor, tracking his movements as he left the main part of the club and towards the stairs. Lionel and Joe had already been given their orders. Bobby wouldn't be able to trust himself if he saw Dicky right now. On the flip side, he enjoyed watching him squirm.

As Dicky walked back down the stairs and exited the club, Bobby watched the girl who had danced with Dicky. She was coming up to the office clutching a phone in her hand.

Joe's voice buzzed through from his earpiece to Bobby's office, "Boss, Rachel says she's got the wanker's phone."

Oh, this will be good! This will be very good indeed. Bobby had hit the jackpot.

"Send the girl in Joe. Come on, don't keep the poor 'thing' waiting." The girl had done her job. Now he could see what Dicky Farrell had really been up to. Rachel stepped into his office. *Yes. She really is quite lovely I suppose*. But as he stared at the girl's face, he saw only Emily.

"Thank you, Rachel, you have done the right thing. We take matters of lost property very seriously here at Blue Tiger. Your vigilance is greatly appreciated," Bobby smiled at the girl who nervously bowed and walked off. As he held the phone it dawned on him that the phone was no doubt locked by a pin-code. It was confirmed to him as he exhausted the most commonly used passwords.

Beep-Beep

It was his lucky day! The phone had received a message and displayed the full contents, meeting place and all and without him needing to open it. The contact name was 'Journo'. Hardly discreet, thought Bobby. This would be very interesting indeed. He couldn't wait to see how this played out.

ALICE

The automatic barrier rolled up after she pulled the plastic-coated card from the unmanned ticket dispenser. Alice was careful to try and hide her face from the cameras as much as possible whilst drawing an arm back into the vehicle and sliding up the electric window. Not being captured on CCTV wasn't entirely essential but the advice was – be as cautious as possible – not any easy task in Bristol but keeping a low profile would be wise. The automatic, innocuous car pulled up the multi-story carpark ramp at pedestrian speed. Alice was keen to keep to the five mile an hour signs dotted through the concrete. Finding the least illuminated space, she parked the car and pulled the woollen hat over her head, making sure to tuck her long corkscrewed dyed blonde hair inside. The look was finished off with a pair of oversized dark sunglasses, a style suited more to sun drenched tourists on a beach than that of these shadows. Satisfied she exited the car and took out the backpack containing her ample belongings and locked the vehicle.

Alice scanned the area for other patrons. The coast was clear. She proceeded to the exit stairs. This procedure had been replicated several times before but never the same car park, never the same lodgings. As far as she was aware she hadn't attracted attention. Years of practice had all but hidden her limp. Alice allowed herself to over play it this time hoping she'd hidden it enough on her last outing.

She checked in to the bed and breakfast, a generic three-story house which had been converted into small individual guest rooms. Her room was typically on the top floor, the steep climb did her aching leg no good, but she decided it was a fair compromise given the privacy it offered. Alice unpacked her bag and changed into a new outfit. She'd tired her wardrobe on the previous visits and had made a mental note to pick up some new clothing from a charity shop to avoid the more securely monitored high street chain stores. Again, this was perhaps a bit too over cautious, but it did no harm to play it safe. The clothes would be returned to another charity once they had served their purpose. During the two-hour drive from home she ignored her rumbling stomach, choosing instead to make good time through the heavy traffic and ignoring the roadside eateries. There was no putting it off any longer. She needed food. Eating at the guest house was not an option as it would encourage more engagement than necessary with other guests or indeed the staff. So, she ventured out into the city centre to find a quiet pub. Heading up Queen Charlotte Street she spotted a busy looking bar, she chanced a look inside but couldn't see any empty tables. Although the rest would have done the ache from her prosthetic leg some good a food vendor would be more discreet, she decided, heading towards St. Nicholas Market. The busy and covered marketplace would provide her with the type of privacy she desired.

Her hunger satisfied by the street food noodle bar (it wasn't great but then she had eaten worse), Alice headed for a vacant taxi giving the driver directions for her chosen destination in Hotwells. The Kurdish driver was thankfully not familiar to her and though he tried his best to start small talk, she kept the conversation to the minimum. They arrived a little way from where she wanted to be, her intention being to walk the rest of the way on foot. Making sure to tip the driver not too much but not too little, remaining as forgettable as possible. All leads led to this despicable being she would be confronting tonight.

After countless failed interviews which had led nowhere. Hundreds of pounds of her own money wasted on bullshit stories, she was trying to source her information from a world that was more tightly knit than a Kevlar vest. But if Alice was right (and she believed she was) then this would be her final journey to this vile underbelly that thrived on the weak and profited from crime. As she reached for the handle the taxi door swung open for her. A well dressed and presentable man in his early fifties held the door open for her, offering his arm.

"Madam," he said with a kind smile.

Unable to respond and with nowhere else to go she accepted the man's hand. He gracefully lifted her out of the car. Alice looked into his sympathetic eyes whilst being led towards an expensive looking black saloon style car. Two very large men who could have passed as master wrestlers stood by the shiny Bentley. The ever so slightly larger of the pair held the door open, patiently.

This wasn't the man Alice had wanted to meet tonight or any other night for that matter. Obviously, she hadn't been careful enough.

"I believe we have a lot to talk about."

***

The handsome and well-dressed gentleman offered his hand to her as the luxurious car pulled away. "Robert Cavendish, but please call me Bobby. It is a pleasure to meet you Madam."

She nervously took his gentle yet firm hand and paused before replying, "…"

"May I be so bold as to ask, who you are Madam? It seems only fair seeing as you have found out so much about me, yet I know so little about you," Cavendish said with the greatest of manners.

Alice knew she had pushed it too far with her digging. Journalist had seemed such a good cover at first. She couldn't turn up playing the distressed mother act (or auntie in her case). Nobody in this runaway's paradise would open themselves up to her for that. Playing the journalist meant being able to offer money and it had worked. He had warned her not to get close to Bobby Cavendish and at first, she had listened. The stories her husband had told her about him had curled her toes. Still, she couldn't let him down. He needed this and she had always felt responsible for the girl *and* her parent's deaths. Still, the more Cavendish's associates and employees talked, the more confidence she gained. If they were happy to spill the beans for a couple hundred pounds a time, then how much did they truly fear the infamous gangster?

That was before Alice Chilcot found herself in a car with him and his thugs.

"I'm erm. I'm Alice Chilcot and I'm looking for a young girl I believe may be working for you called Hannah. I'm her auntie you see. The thing is and I do hope I won't be getting anybody into trouble, but I've been… well, advised by some of your employees that she may be going under the name Emily…here I can show you a photo…"

Bobby had to smile. Bloody journalist! She had him worried there for a while but here it was, just another concerned family member. He had been right to wait with this one. It was a shame he had to let so many of his girls go now. That didn't matter now though, because right in front of him was a golden opportunity to make a good impression with the beautiful girl's family! This was working out very well indeed.

"Lionel, please take Mrs Chilcot and I to the Opa," he called to the driver.

"My dear, let's celebrate! We have much to talk about."

Lionel pulled the car up to the front of the exclusive restaurant. Alice was heavily relieved that they were at a public place but her confusion to Cavendish's reaction to her truth was unsettling. The driver got out of his seat with surprising fluidness despite his huge bulk and opened her door offering his hand to Alice. Swinging her good leg on to the pavement. There was a tiny moment to consider if she should try to run, until the other equally large bodyguard's phone started to ring. Lionel withdrew his hand and waited for the other heavy to answer. Bobby himself pulled his legs back inside the car.

"Yeah…now?... No. More time. NO! More time… CUNT!" The second man threw the phone down and began smashing it into small pieces with his ginormous foot.

"Boss, we need to go," he looked over to Lionel nodding towards Alice.

"Get her in, let's go!"

Lionel motioned with the door for Alice to put her good leg back into the car. The beef cakes quickly jumped into their seats in front and they took off with speed.

"What the fuck is going on Joe?!" Cavendish screamed from the back seat as the car drifted around the corner of a busy street into the wrong lane.

"Police have got a warrant for your arrest Boss." Joe motioned to Alice and then gave Bobby a look of wariness.

"Don't fucking worry about that Joe! Spit it out!"

"It's that girl you been looking for Boss. They found her dead. They say they've got something on you."

Cavendish put it all together in his mind.

"That fucker Dicky! I knew he had something to do with it!" Bobby had ignored the gut feelings, but now he knew the girl hadn't left of her own free will. The problem was it wasn't Dicky sitting in a car with the recent deceased's auntie. Alice interrupted his thoughts.

"Dick... Dicky Farrell?" Alice's voice wavered. Surely, they weren't talking about Hannah. But then this Dicky Farrell was meant to be her boyfriend according to the girls she had spoken with. At the very least her sources ended with him being the last reported person to see her alive. It was the man she had expected to meet tonight.

Cavendish looked back at that woman. What was he going to do with her? His life was over. There was no going back, he would have to cover his tracks even if it meant killing his darling Emily's family. Alice sensing this look in

Bobby's eyes and her own mix of fear and suspected grief, decided to play her wild card.

"Mr Cavendish. My husband is DCI Chilcot and I believe we could help each other."

PART TWO

PERFECT PICTURE CARD SCENE

Another single carriage A-road and he knew the all too familiar city life was behind him. He had no love for the M25 or any of its connecting arteries, but it beat the monotonous stop start traffic jams of the A303. Rubber-necking-motorhomes and on-tow caravans ogling Stonehenge. He couldn't understand it's attraction, a pile of ancient bricks he'd been convincing himself had been placed for the sole purpose of congesting his access to the Southwest of England. The modern world had mastered the art of building giant skyscrapers that jutted into the skyline, miles of underground railways that carefully and successfully navigated through Victorian drain routes, foundations and yet here he was apparently the only person in a fifty mile stretch who could see it for what it was: A bunch of rocks. The drive was only made worse by his decision to make the journey on a bank holiday weekend. He hadn't had any choice but to make a short visit back to the house he had reluctantly inherited from his mother in Barkingside, London, before he was due to start his new job in the Southwest of England. A small town, Colney, of which he'd never heard of until his recent misfortune had taken his career on an unexpected U-turn.

He had spent the last decade of his career in Bristol where he'd built somewhat of a comfortable life, but then an abrupt decision had landed him with a relocation via the M4 to collect his personal belongings in the capital. That's why he now found himself stuck in traffic alongside the weekend tourists.

He lifted his left foot to the biting point of the clutch to fill the space the motorhome in front had offered him. His Lexus edged forward before coming to another grounding halt. Looking out of his passenger window he saw a family of strawberry sellers wearing hi-vis vests and holding handwritten signs.

Strawberries £2 a punnet!

They were moving down the rows of traffic, approaching the windows, attempting to sell the pallets to imprisoned motorists. He accidentally caught the attention of a cheery looking pig-tailed teen who, after making eye contact and believing she had found a customer, approached his car window. She bent down slightly to his height and made a knocking gesture with her fist towards his window. He shook his head at the girl, but she refused to move and held up her basket of ripe fruit. This time he paid her no extra curtesy and extended his middle finger. To his pleasure the young girl's jaw drooped open in stunned expression, he found the look wasn't too dissimilar to that of the excited tourists who had gaped at Stonehenge only moments ago. The motorhome pulled forward allowing him to pull his Lexus forward a few feet. The car pulled away leaving the girl shocked, standing frozen with her basket of strawberries. Looking into his rear-view mirror he watched the girl approach another one of the strawberry sellers. An older man with a grizzled beard and tight-fitting vest that did little to hide the obvious bulging mass of upper body strength that could only be obtained by a lifetime of graft. The girl pointed out the Lexus to the man, possibly her father. The driver was about to put the car into second gear and move out of the uncomfortable distance when the motor home in front of him stopped sharply and turned on its hazard lights.

They had only moved about fifteen feet away from the now disgruntled male companion. "Shit" he murmured as the unit-of-a-man dropped his fruit basket and marched to the passenger side of his Lexus. Two passengers got out of the motor home ahead of him. One of them waved him in, indicating they needed help pushing the vehicle off the road as it had clearly broken down. The man ignored the two passengers and looked back to the approaching and aggrieved presumably father of the young strawberry seller. A few cars in the line of traffic behind him had begun to see an opportunity to get ahead and were making manoeuvres to overtake the Lexus and the stationary motorhome but the driver hadn't left himself enough space to overtake. He put the car into reverse as the stunned passengers in need of assistance stared back at him, appalled that no assistance was coming their way. Hemmed in by the cars behind trying to filter past the obstruction, and inside the Lexus, he ignored the meaty fists of the male strawberry seller now knocking on his passenger window. He kept inching back to the hoots of the car behind who also had nowhere to go but was still trying to find his own gap to get past the broken-down motorhome. Sensing that the driver was not about to give up the safety of his car the male strawberry seller started to exchange words with the two passengers of the motorhome who were now looking at the trapped driver with some disgust. Finally, the other car behind had managed to reverse a foot or so. This gave the man all the space he needed to angle his car around the motorhome.

He floored the Lexus forward but not before the leather boot of the unhappy seller had indented the passenger door. He narrowly missed a collision with another car from the oncoming traffic which screamed its horn, he returned the favour whilst adding a fist in a wanking gesture to the stunned old lady driving.

Narrowly escaping the confrontation, hoping that no one had taken his registration details. In the end it wouldn't matter but it was just the sort of incident he could avoid right now.

As a result of his recent distress, he thought it was long overdue for a little perk me up. The traffic had been moving at a steady pace for the last few miles, he was well shot of the confrontation, a service station was shown on the road sign for the next junction. He pulled off and parked his car at the roadside cafe. Entering the restaurant he found himself queuing, all families with wailing children waiting to be seated. As he joined the que another family filed in behind him. The mother was dragging a small screaming boy of about six years old behind her promising him a toy from the merchandise stall if he behaved and ate his dinner first. The other child presumably a slightly older sister, was enjoying her younger siblings' meltdown and was tormenting the child with taunts of cry-baby. The boy started pushing his sister to more outcries from the mother, meanwhile the dad continued to keep his face glued to his phone. He tried to ignore their family as the people ahead of him were slowly filtered through to their plastic tables. He could feel his temper rising. The sister amplified the situation and with a mischievous look in her eye pushed her brother again, making the boy lose his footing and crash into him.

Parochial Pigs

"Polly, stop winding up your bother!" the mother said through gritted teeth, clearly trying to avoid making a further scene.

"Simon, will you put your phone down and help me with your bloody kids."

The phone-engrossed father looked down and surveyed the situation. Looking from his children to his wife, confused as to why he had been torn away from his game of candy crush.

"Polly just pushed Thomas into that man ahead," she exclaimed to her husband.

"Polly darling don't push your brother," was his best response.

He was simmering with anger; he just could not abide rudeness.

It was up there with his pet peeves in life, alongside screaming children.

"Yeah don't worry about it, its fine!" he muttered to the father of the boy.

The father shared a shocked glance with his wife. It wasn't their little angel of a child that had been rude but the not-so-innocent- bystander. He rolled his eyes and returned them to his phone. Now at bursting point, as he was summoning up what would be his best response, the waitress returned to the please-wait-to-be-seated podium and said to the man, "How many seats do you need sir?"

"Just me."

In all the family activity he hadn't noticed the waitress. She looked to be young twenties if not a bit younger without all that make up. She had long blonde hair tied in a ponytail and a tiny waist, the man didn't hide his intrusive look at the young girl's large breasts. As he gave her a purposeful look up and down one of the little brats behind him, the sister, let forth an ear-splitting shriek befitting of an amputation without anaesthetic.

"Ouch! Mummy, Thomas pinched me!" and descended into wailing tears.

The waitress looked pass the man as she spoke, "We have a table for four ready Madam, would you and your family like to take that now? I'm sure this gentleman wouldn't mind waiting would you Sir?" The waitress looked at the man with an obvious look of self- accomplishment.

The man hadn't noticed the waitress' look of disgust (he was somewhat distracted by her physique in any case). This was just her power trip he thought. He would let her have it.

"I have been waiting longer, sweet cheeks," he replied.

"We are just clearing a two-seater for you now sir, I'm sure you won't have to wait much longer. My colleague will be over to show you to your table soon."

The young waitress turned her back on him with an obviously fake smile that he thought perhaps actually meant 'Fuck you' and showed the family to their seats. He watched with stunned disbelief at the family expecting at least a thanks from the parents but all he received was a stuck-out tongue from the young girl named 'Poppy.' With the parent's and waitresses' backs turned the man mouthed the words "little

Parochial Pigs

shit" to the girl who turned to her thankfully preoccupied mother and tried to explain but it was received by deaf ears from either parent. They were clearly just relieved to get to the table. Pepper Pig was already being readied on the dad's phone screen.

Another waitress came to the waiting sign and told the man his table was ready. This waitress, to his disappointment, was much older than the other girl and much larger. He didn't hide his disgust in her.

A full English breakfast laced with a secret sauce of saliva from the aggrieved waitresses. He washed it down with two cups of black coffee. It was a good start, but he was long overdue a top up – he took himself to the little boy's room. The toilets had seen better days. Cheap reformed wood panelling covered with a shiny veneer of laminate. It went without saying that the door locks had been missing for some time. He checked all the cubicles in the yellow glow of the lights for their vacancy. There was a huge turd in one of the pans, though none of that really mattered – he was just glad they were empty of people. He took the last one in a row of three and stuffed the door a jamb with wadded up tissue to stop it from swinging open. He read the common place scribble of "call for a good time" and wondered if he should make a mental note of the number for later. Instead, he removed his wallet producing a small Sealey bag of cocaine, his credit card and a twenty-pound note. After pouring out a healthy portion on top of the porcelain cistern and separating the pile of white powder into two fat lines he rolled up the twenty and hoovered up the first line.
As he let the mix of powder and mucus slide down his throat,

he heard the toilets main door open. He froze at the male voice.

"Go in that cubicle Thomas, Daddy will be in the one next to you."

He quickly packed up the little baggy and credit card, deciding to dab the remaining powder with his finger. What he hadn't realised was that the door to the cubicle stood wide open and the young boy from the queue earlier was standing in the doorway. The boy's feet were firmly planted to the floor as his eyes stared with curiosity at the cistern lid.

"What's that?" the little boy asked with a cheeky grin. The man spun round and smiled as he saw the boy.

"Sherbet," he whispered, "It's all for you, and don't tell your sister!" pocketing his wallet and leaving the second line of cocaine on the toilet cistern. He side stepped the little boy who was already taking a step into the cubicle and as he left the toilets, he heard the dad say from behind the other closed cubicle, "Who are you talking to Thomas?"

The man promptly paid his bill at the counter not waiting for the beast to return with the receipt. The curvy one was waiting at the till. Her face contorted into what he believed was meant to be a smile but had such a forced look that even he knew it.

"Was everything okay for you today sir?"

"Err, yeah. Just want to pay my bill."

The waitress put his money through the till and gave him his change. He hovered his hand over the tip pot for just a split second before depositing the coins in his pocket. The waitress watched him leave pleased she'd included the extra ingredient in his food. Quickly starting the ignition of the Lexus, he pulled out of the car park wondering what he'd give to be a fly on the car window for the family's long journey home.

James Jenkins

RED MIST

The buzz from his earlier sniff at the Roadside Cafe toilet was beginning to fade. He entered what his sat nav had him believe was the final part of his journey. There hadn't been *anything* in the last thirty miles that resembled a town. Roads wound up and down across fields, that had now given way to tight country lanes. The only landmarks being the undressed stone flint houses that barely populated the area. The sun would break suddenly when the trees thinned out, temporarily blinding him, which only served to piss him off more, reminding him that he had left his Gucci sunglasses back in London. He'd planned to pick up a cheap pair from the service station but after his 'encounter', he'd forgot. He didn't think he would be finding many places around here to buy booze let alone sunglasses. What was this shit hole? He made another left turn as instructed by the crap sat nav only to find himself stuck behind a slow-moving Toyota Yaris. What was it about the Yaris that attracted that type of non-urgency in a driver? He could imagine them having an owner's club where they meet up regularly (probably in a coffee shop, as they were too responsible to drive to a pub and enjoy a half glass of shandy), he could imagine their self- satisfaction and back slaps from the likeminded twats they congregated with. The sort of individuals that you see in small hamlets volunteering to use handheld speed cameras on their day off to catch mildly speeding fellow motorists. "Fuck off!" he shouted to no one. He thought he recognised a sign he'd already passed but it was just another of the many handwritten 'Scrumpy for sale next left!', 'local honey here!', 'Eggs. A dozen for a pound!' Signs, apparently that were in abundance throughout the area. Finally letting his predictably short patience get the better of him he pulled alongside the pitiful car on the almost single file road and began beeping his horn to get the driver's attention. The Yaris driver made a motion with their hands indicating that he should just overtake but this was not the agitated man's perception of the gesture – his misconception escalated his already volatile mood, now very much in need of another sniff of nose candy. It was not uncommon for him to reach this level of fury: he was very much aware of the warning signs himself. People had always warned him about his irrational split-second decisions he was oh so prone to make – he took note of it, he really did. He knew the outcomes of these moments rarely worked out for him despite his timeless efforts to get himself out of trouble, using *every* means available to him. He was always trying to take control of these mood swings, but when he was on the final vinegar strokes of a coke high it was usually past his own ability to control altogether. This was one of those times. Slamming his foot on the accelerator and swinging the car to the right with all the driving prowess of a seventeen-year-old-twat in a one litre Corsa at an afterhours supermarket car park, he pulled alongside the car. The little car appeared to be increasing in speed for perhaps its first time ever, this forced the Lexus to have to speed up further still. From around the blind corner ahead he saw a large delivery van heading towards him and with the distance becoming worryingly shorter by the nanosecond. He stamped on the brake pedal and pulled the car back in behind the little Toyota, failing to see the large and unforgiving tractor that had caught up to them and was now filling the void he had formerly occupied. To make things even worse the stupid car in front was now decreasing its speed. He hoped he'd guessed the gap right as the tractor blared out its painfully loud horn. He could see from the rear-view mirror that the agricultural behemoth was braking incredibly hard, but the tractor just kept coming. To his gratitude it finally came to a halt, but not before hitting the boot of the car and jarring his back. He swung the driver's door open and jumped out swearing at the tractor driver as he surveyed the broken rear lights and crumpled boot. The Toyota Yaris carried on ahead seemingly unaware of the destruction it had left behind in its wake. He put his hands up to his head cursing and kicked his door shut in anger. The tractor driver leapt down from his cab, a red-faced man easily in his late fifties and well over six feet. Despite his age and dungarees, the other man ceased his hissy fit and stared at the farmer with trepidation.

"What the bloody hell are you doing?" the farmer barked in a thick West Country accent, "These things don't stop as quickly as your fancy car you bloody twerp!"

As the farmer shouted this last part out, spittle flying from his mouth, the man was very much beginning to regret the collision and though he had to admit he could have handled things better, he still had no intention of backing down. The farmer could argue it as much as he wanted but the law would protect the driver in front. He knew this, it's not like there were any witnesses that had stuck around on this road of back and beyond. He was fucking big though this farmer, those meaty fists looked like a couple of JCB buckets. However, he still had an ace up his sleeve.

The farmer started to take a mobile phone from his pocket, presumably with the intention of taking the car driver's details. The situation had taken an unexpected turn for him. Clearly the farmer was a law-abiding citizen, the fear of an arse kicking evaporating he began to try and turn this mishap in his favour.

"Wouldn't do that if I were you mate, you should have stopped in time," he said whilst grabbing the farmer's phone from his hand.

"That's bloody theft that is! What's this all about? You one of them whiplash claimants or something?"

He could see the farmer was obviously shaken up. He had to laugh to himself – this old boy was probably capable of wrestling a bull. Removing his own mobile phone, he started to take pictures of the tractor and his beloved Lexus with the now crumpled boot. He would deal with the farmer in a minute, for now he was nervously trying to cover himself. Clearly the situation had escalated to something he didn't need especially considering his recent circumstances. He was also keen to avoid any more motoring offences after his previous incident on the A303. It might have been easier to take the beating instead.

"What the bloody hell are you playing at? I'll have you know I'm on very good terms with the local police chief around here."

"Not good enough I'd say mate..." as he pulled his wallet from his pocket, shoving it under the nose of the unsuspecting farmer.

"Sergeant Paul Hargreaves!"

The obviously rehearsed and smug way to which the man produced his identification had taken the farmer off guard. As soon as he had identified himself all aggression escaped the older man. This gave Hargreaves a great deal of satisfaction.

"Oh, my, I, err. I didn't realise officer."

"Sir, you have interrupted the work of an on-duty policeman," he lied.

"Hang on a minute Officer, I clearly had no idea you were a policeman, surely you can see this was an accident."

"Never mind the collision mate. But were you not aware of the uneven load you are carrying on your trailer?"

Hargreaves had noticed the hay when he took the pictures. The load had become precarious due to the collision with Sergeant Hargreaves' Lexus. Normally he wouldn't have bothered, but if any of the past few weeks had taught the sergeant anything then it was to make sure his shit didn't stink. If it meant threatening this hillbilly farmer into submission using the full extent of the law, then he had no qualms about doing that.

"Uneven load?! You must be bloody joking! It was fine before you skidded to a halt in front of me!"

"Swearing at an officer won't help you here sir."

Paul Hargreaves moved swiftly grabbing the farmer by his wrist and bending it behind his back. Hargreaves enjoyed the unnecessary and excessive force. The man shouted in obvious discomfort before yielding to the officer. He'd judged the farmer's reaction perfectly.

"Sorry Officer, please it was my mistake."

Hargreaves wanted to keep bending the bigger man's arm back until it snapped or to get him to cough up a bit of financial compensation but with his anger residing, he began to remember something the farmer had said back in the heat of the moment. With his vain need for respect restored he relinquished the man's hand and composed himself.

"Did you say you knew the local police chief round here?"

"Err, yes. Yes, I do, I'm proud to count him as a good friend of mine," the farmer replied whilst massaging his recently liberated arm.

"DCI Chilcot?" Paul asked.

"Why yes! That's him."

"Looks like it's your day then pal."

Paul thanked his lucky stars. Breaking your new boss' friends' arm before he'd even started was not going to be a good start. Bribery wouldn't go down any better either. Time to turn on some of the old Hargreaves charm.

"Sergeant Paul Hargreaves." He extended his right hand to the farmer who looked at it as if he was awaiting a trick. The older man looked at Paul's smiling face before gingerly accepting it.

"Colney's new police sergeant, Sorry if we got off on the wrong foot back then mate."

"I err, I'm Donovan McKay but everyone calls me Don. Yes indeed. Me too Sergeant, how very embarrassing. The whole town has been very much looking forward to meeting our new member of the police force. Wait until I tell my Delores about this."

This was going very nicely, Paul decided. After what he had just put the farmer through the local man would be bang to rights shouting about police brutality and corruption. The farmer now seemed genuinely remorseful.

"Well Don, how about you escort your new best friend here to Colney town centre?" Hmm? Was that pushing it he wondered. He'd been told he was a condescending prick before.

"Oh, I'd be honoured Sergeant!"

Really? Paul thought. This bloke was too easy.

"There is just a small matter of the damage to the car though," Paul said with a mock wince looking at the tractor rear ending his precious Lexus.

"No problem at all... err, Paul, was it?"

"Sergeant Hargreaves," Paul corrected.

"Oh yes, of course. Sorry. Sergeant if you allow me to sort it out for you, I will have my brother look at your car. He has a colleague at his garage who specialises in body work repairs. Please let me take care of this for you and maybe we can keep this whole incident between ourselves."

This was working out very nicely for Hargreaves indeed.

"Any good?" he quizzed – "This brother's mate of yours I mean?"

"Oh yes! I would swear by him Sergeant. My farm is on the way into Colney. If you like, you are welcome to bring it to mine. I'll have my brother, Jon, pick it up for you from there."

Jon and Don. You couldn't make it up. This all sounded a good idea to Paul, he wouldn't need his car much now, as it was. His recently demoted rank meant a squad car, with all its glorious livery, would be available to him anyway. The Lexus would only be for his own private use.

"I can give you a lift into the town centre once we've dropped off your car, although it's not a far walk if you'd prefer?"

"Lift would be good, thank you Don."

After separating the vehicles from each other Paul allowed the tractor to pull in front of him and followed at a calmer pace. Although things hadn't turned out too badly in the end, it had still postponed any possible coke breaks and he was badly beginning to feel the need for a drink – or ten. He started to massage his temples, considering if he could fish the stash out the glovebox when the tractor slowed and started indicating to the left. Hargreaves followed the tractor off the main road and onto a gravelled and rutted track. As more parts from the rear of the Lexus continued to be rattled off, Paul gritted his teeth and hoped the farmer's brothers' friend was as good as he was made out to be. The gravel track took them uphill before reaching a peak and winding back down, revealing a modest sized farmhouse that was encompassed by some outer buildings and a large barn. A border collie was barking and wagging its tail as it ran up to the tractor. "Great" Paul said to himself. He wasn't an animal person. From an early age he'd always sensed that animals didn't like him. From an early age he'd known the feeling was mutual.

The tractor pulled up to the large barn and Donovan McKay jumped out. He patted the dog, then motioned to Paul to pull his car up by the house. He did as he was instructed and parked the car before stepping out.

"Welcome to my home Sergeant Hargreaves," Don said, dramatically motioning his arms towards the ancient buildings. "Don't mind Lass here, she's a working dog but she does love a little bit of fuss."

Paul stared at the dog already standing a half step behind its owner and beginning to let out a low guttural growl.

"No! Stop it! Shu!" The dog responded to her owner, running off towards the outer reaches of the buildings. Paul sighed with relief; he had no desire to make nice with a mangey farm dog that was probably covered in pig shit.

"So sorry, Sergeant. I don't know what come over her. She's never done that before."

"It's not a problem really." Paul really wasn't worried.

"Come inside please, I'll give my brother a quick call and let him know the car's here. Fancy a quick brew before I drop you in town Sergeant?"

Paul could go for a coffee. He still had his hip flask with him and if he was going to have to sit in that tractor with Don, then he might need a little drop. He always found it more sociably accepting to drink in the day if it wasn't totally neat.

"Coffee would be lovely cheers."

"Please have a seat Sergeant," Don said motioning towards the large pine dining table that occupied the centre of the farmhouse kitchen. Paul pulled out one of the chairs, scraping it along the stone floor. The farmer filled the kettle

Parochial Pigs

up from the sink faucet and placed it back in its electrical holder. Paul couldn't help feeling the modern kettle was out of place in the period kitchen's décor. He expected an old kettle whistling on top of the ancient AGA. It was already beginning to hiss and distil, his ears barely coping.

"Will you be staying with us long term in Colney, Sergeant?"

"Hopefully not. No offence, but I'm not a big fan of the country life. My skills are more akin to catching *serious* criminals in urban crime areas."

"Sounds like you were quite the policeman back in... where is it you came from Sergeant?" Don asked as he pulled the now boiled kettle from its plug and started pouring the steaming liquid into a cup.

"Bristol. I'm from London originally but I moved to Bristol as soon as I could get a transfer."

"London? Really? I can't say I'm a big fan myself, but why the need for such drastic relocation?"

"There was nothing there for me anymore."

The farmer placed the hot black coffee in a chipped mug in front of Paul. Paul cast his mind back to his final year in London. He'd watched the life drain from the skeletal husk of that wicked woman who once was his mother. It was a rare happy memory of his early years of life in the capital. Suddenly he snapped his mind back from this bittersweet chapter of his past, the farmer had been saying something to Paul.

"Are you ok Sergeant? Was it something I said?"

"No, just a bit tired is all. Been a busy few days. What were you saying?"

"Milk? Sugar? Can I offer you a biscuit? I think Delores has some chocolate Hob-Nobs here somewhere."

"The Coffee's fine as it is, thanks." Hargreaves reached to his breast pocket for his hip flask before remembering he had left his suit jacket in the Lexus. Armani suit of course. He wouldn't have had it any other way.

"Err, you wouldn't have anything a little bit stronger? Just a little drop to perk me up you know?"

"Oh yes. Let me grab something for you Sergeant."

The big man went to one of the pine cupboards and rummaged around briefly before pulling out a glass bottle, its label had long faded.

"Here we go Sergeant. Fine Scotch Whiskey, Single malt. I don't touch the stuff myself anymore but please be my guest," he said as he unscrewed the cap and began to pour the contents into the coffee mug. "Say when…"

Paul allowed the whiskey to brim the top of the cup before saying, "…When."

Don put the bottle back into the cupboard, Paul storing a mental note of its location.

"You enjoy your drink and I'll just give my brother a call about your car. Once I've taken the trailer off the tractor I'll come back and get you so we can get on our way to town. You just make yourself at home Sergeant Hargreaves."

Paul nodded as the farmer exited back through the big farmhouse door, letting the afternoon sunshine pour across the room.

James Jenkins

KEEPSAKE

Hargreaves, as ever, greedily slurped at the boozy coffee, savouring the fumes as the relief of the alcohol burnt down through to his stomach. He finished the drink within four mouthfuls and welcomed the slight stirring of a buzz within. That's a good start, he thought, still yearning for more, but all that coffee from the service station had swelled his bladder. Wondering if he should wait for the farmer to return before exploring for a toilet, he considered the hospitable man's words: "Make yourself at home," Paul would do just that. After all, he had been invited in and he was an officer of the law. Policemen were like vampires in that respect, once you invited them in... and Paul considered that he would quite like the idea of being a vampire.

He stood up from the uneven but solid pine chair and headed towards the far kitchen door which led into the heart of the property. The door had one of those latches you operated with your thumb. He opened it and stepped into a hallway which had a staircase at one end and two doors leading to other rooms on the ground floor. Paul passed a small table in the hall where a landline phone sat neatly on a doily cloth. Maybe the farmer was using his mobile to call his brother he wondered away. Uninterested anyway, Paul started towards the stairs deciding to have a 'little nose' while he was about. He reached the top of the carpeted stairs and walked out on to a long narrow landing where two doors stood on either side of the landing. As he walked along the corridor, the walls of which displayed pictures of painted horses and landscapes, he thought he could hear some movement from one of the rooms. Not wanting to be caught snooping he tried the first door on the right, which as it turned out, was a large bathroom. The slanted ceiling was held up by exposed wooden beams. Apart from the basin and toilet he saw, there was a cast iron roll top bath standing in one corner. Hargreaves had never been a lover of anything set in this prehistoric style. Why anyone would choose this over clean modern acrylic he never knew. Regardless he pushed back the toilet seat and released the contents of his bladder. The overdue toilet break causing his stream of piss to miss the bowl on his first attempt. He wouldn't be cleaning it up. Shaking himself dry he then turned his attention to the second and perhaps most important bit of business. Unlike the hip flask, he had at least, remembered to bring the class A drug in with him. He closed the seat, not out of any common curtesy but purely out of fear of knocking anything off the top of the cistern into the bowl beneath. What did that feng shui bollocks tell you? Always close your toilet seat to stop your wealth flushing away. He spread out the powder and cut a healthy line, making up for the one he'd so kindly given away earlier. The powder shot up his nose and into his blood stream, causing his eyes to water in pleasure. "That's the one Pauly boy!" he said to himself in the pewter edged mirror. He packed his contraband back into his pockets and walked over to the bathroom window, taking in the view of the desolated farm. He could see the farmer struggling with the trailer down by the barn, some of the load had fallen off and was now being tossed back by the massive farmer's bulking pitchfork. Paul guessed that he had a few minutes to himself as he turned his mind back to the whiskey bottle in the kitchen cupboard. Just about to turn around the bathroom door swung open.

Clearly Paul had failed to notice the little latch that would have secured the door shut. He guessed this was Delores, the farmer's wife. The door swung fully open revealing a pretty girl with long dark hair, her voluptuous figure amplified by the loosely wrapped bath towel. Not noticing the stranger in her bathroom, she began to let the towel slip down to her waist before looking up at a frozen Paul Hargreaves who was staring lecherously at her now revealed left breast. Hargreaves couldn't drag his eyes away from the perked tit with its pink and erect nipple. The girl let out a loud scream before pulling her towel back around herself.

"Who the fucking hell are you?!" she demanded, catching the sergeant's perverted eyes.

"Sergeant Paul Hargreaves," he extended a hand, barely able to contain his excitement of the unexpected situation. One that most men would have recoiled in embarrassment from. Not Paul though. The girl looked down from his eyes to his visibly swollen groin ignoring the outstretched hand. Not only because she was still in shock but also because it would mean releasing her towel again, something she was beginning to sense the sergeant would welcome.

"I'm a guest of Don's... Who do I have the honour of meeting here?"

He still hadn't made any attempt to leave the bathroom clearly making the girl feel deeply uncomfortable.

"I'm Milly, Don is my dad. Why didn't you lock the fucking door you twat?"

"Now Milly, that's no way to talk to a policeman, is it? I'm sure your dad won't appreciate that foul language either.

Exposing yourself to an officer too!" he cackled to his own amusement.

"You're a policeman?" She could hardly believe it. Wondering if her abrupt reaction to him might have been better considered.

Hargreaves stepped towards the girl and squeezed through the doorway before she could step out of the way. He made a point of brushing his genitals against her thigh as he did.

"Lovely to meet to meet you Milly, maybe I'll see you again soon," Paul whispered in the girl's ear. The mixture of coffee breath, whiskey and cocaine-induced saliva made her gag. She stepped into the bathroom, slamming the door behind her. Hargreaves smiled to himself. The girl was only playing hard to get. Maybe this Colney place wouldn't be too bad after all. And this girl Millie, though perhaps a bit young for Paul as a man of thirty-four. He pegged the girl at around her very late teens, perhaps early twenties and as it's said, if there's grass on the wicket…

Hargreaves massaged his erect cock through his suit trousers, he knew it would have to wait and in any case one of the doors were ajar. Presumably this being the room the farmer's daughter had come from. He slowly crept along the landing and pushed the door open. Glancing around the room he took note of the décor. Fan posters of some heavily tattooed rapper adorned the walls. Paul was trying to work out if the girl was, perhaps, a bit old for such juvenile pictures when something else caught his eye, distracting him from the information his brain had been putting together. Bingo! He had hit the jackpot. Hanging over the top of the laundry bin were a pair of white panties. Nothing too special but Hargreaves picked up the knickers and breathed in the girl's scent – the messages to his penis threatening to burst from his Versace trousers. He pocketed them and slipped back out of the room, as he walked past the bathroom, disappointed that there was a lack of a keyhole in the door. Still, he had a lovely little souvenir and surely the farmer wouldn't be much longer. He didn't want to push his luck. Hargreaves went down the stairs to the kitchen. He was deliberating having a quick swig of the whiskey when Don came back through the door.

"Sorry to keep you Sergeant, I'm ready now though if you want to make a move?"

"No problem at all Don, I had to find your toilet, but the lovely Milly showed me to the bathroom. Lovely lady you've raised there I must say."

"You must be honoured Sergeant. I'm surprised she even came out of her room to greet you. A rare privilege indeed."

Hargreaves followed the farmer through the kitchen door thankful that his bulging tent pole had now subsided. They walked over to the Lexus so Paul could grab his belongings. He opened the crumpled boot – the last of the glass from the lights jettisoned from the fixings as he slammed it, unsuccessfully, shut again.

"I've spoken to my brother; he is coming along later this evening with his friend to pick your car up Sergeant. He said he will let you know when it's ready. Have you got a place to stay in town then?"

For a minute Paul thought the farmer was going to offer him a place at the farm to stay. He wouldn't mind a night under the same roof as the beautiful Milly. Who knew what opportunities might present themselves? She may be a tough nut to crack but Paul had usually found that sometimes, two ways into a girl's pants were the police badge and the drugs. Hargreaves had them both, the latter in abundance.

"The Sunny Inn or something like that I think, it's on the sat nav."

"You must mean The Sunyetson Inn! Maggie's place. Oh, well I can promise that you will be in good hands Sergeant. A fine woman is our Maggie."

"You know where it is?" Paul asked as a Land Rover not too old, covered in dust and mud, came down the gravel driveway.

"That I do and what good timing too, here is my dear wife, Delores. She will be so glad she got to meet you. That saves squeezing us both into the tractor's cab no less."

Paul was relieved of that. The Land Rover pulled up beside the two men and a plumb short lady with a friendly face bounced out from the driver's seat. She and her husband shared a brief hug before the farmer introduced the guest to his wife.

"Sergeant Paul Hargreaves, newest member of the esteemed DCI Chilcot's Colney police force!"

"Hello there Paul!" The stumpy lady pulled Hargreaves in for a bear like hug before he could even correct her on his preferred title. His face was forced into the older lady's neck, his nose pushed directly into the folds of fat. Hargreaves had difficulty with fat people, the smell of them disgusted him. He had to endure twenty-three miserable years before the cancer had finally stripped the meat from his mothers' bones. Although he supposed the smell had only worsened. She released him before grabbing his cheeks with both hands, an act she carried out with excited affection.

"Sergeant, Delores! Please," the farmer corrected his wife.

Hargreaves studied the wife. Although she was a cheery woman who may have been more attractive in her early years Paul still couldn't see how she had sired the stunning Milly.

"Its fine madam. Call me Paul, please." He could see the small look of hurt that Don showed on his face and took a tiny bit of pleasure from it.

"Oh no, Sergeant. No, I am happy to show my respect to an officer of the law. Anyone who works for Charlie Chilcot must be quite a policeman, I'm sure. Oh, we do love our police chief. He does so much for the community he does. He graces us with his company almost every Sunday lunch for one of my famous roasts. Oh Mr Hargrea… Sorry, Sergeant Hargreaves, you must join us one time. It would be our pleasure!"

"I'm not too sure the good sergeant will be with us for very long dear," Don informed his wife. "The sergeant hopes to return to the city life once his work here is done."

"Even more reason to make sure you don't leave it too long Sergeant. Once you've got yourself settled in, we will see when you are available."

"Thank you, Delores," Paul said with his best forced smile.

"Come on now Delores let the Sergeant go, he's had a busy day and I'm going to drive him into town."

"Of course, of course do forgive me Sergeant. Don is always telling me I go on too much. Oh, but where are you staying Sergeant Hargreaves?"

"He's staying at Maggie's," the farmer replied for him.

"Let the sergeant speak for himself dear. Oh, but anyway Sergeant you will be in great hands with Maggie! Rest assured."

The kindly lady grabbed Paul back in for another crushing embrace before releasing him slightly winded.

"Lovely to meet you, Sergeant."

"You too Madam." Paul picked up his cases and walked toward the boot of the Land Rover, Delores clicking it open from the button on her key. Hargreaves loaded as the wife and husband exchanged looks.

"Where's Lass, Don luv?"

"Why I don't know dear, she's normally the first to greet anyone coming up the track. She was behaving strangely earlier."

"Well, she will be back when it's time for her dinner that I'm sure," Delores said before waving to the men and heading towards the farmhouse. Hargreaves and Don jumped into the vehicle, driving back out of the gravel track that joined the main road. The light was beginning to give way to dusk now and Paul was feeling the rumble in his belly calling for food. They drove towards the town, becoming more visible now.

Open fields began to give way to residential areas and randomly scattered older buildings, they passed a local hardware store and next to it a petrol station. Hargreaves didn't recognise the name on the sign above it, assuming it was independently owned he hoped this wasn't the case for every business here. The farmer was pointing out the odd landmark and telling Paul about the local area and amenities, but he barely took any notice. He was feeling tired now and already coming down from his most recent high, quicker than usual but he put this down to his accelerated blood supply pumping around his nether regions back at the farmer's house. He put his hand into his trouser pocket squeezing the cotton underwear. Suddenly the Land Rover pulled up outside a large stone building with a long gravel driveway. A huge weeping willow tree dominated the front garden, covering the path like a tunnel. The sign in the front garden advertised it as a luxury guest house. Paul thought it reminded him of Fawlty Towers and fully expected the same eccentric treatment that was famously dished out by the calamitous owner.

"Here we are Sergeant."

They both got out of the vehicle, Don went to the back of the car and released the boot so Paul could get his belongings.

"Thank you, Don. And please, just call me Paul."

THE FOX

Hargreaves walked up to the oak reception counter. The whole place was heavily in need of modernisation. There was a musty aroma that he hoped didn't extend to the bedrooms. All the pictures and ornaments in the foyer looked like they would fetch a pretty penny on the antiques road show! Random teapots, vases and mantel clocks amongst other dusty artefacts. He never understood people's desires to spend ridiculous amounts of cash on someone else's rubbish. Paul Hargreaves had never been a sentimental man. He noticed a stuffed fox sat upon the reception counter, its fur had begun to thin out in places and the sight of it made Hargreaves' stomach turn. He wouldn't be surprised if this was in fact the source of the foul odour of which he was currently enduring. The fox made about as much sense to him as the scarecrow that had been staked into the front garden of the guest house, most of the houses they had driven past on the way to the inn had them too. Something told Paul he wasn't going to have a lot in common with his new neighbours. He rang the bell on the reception counter. After what was a completely unacceptable amount of time for Hargreaves, an older lady with a short bob wearing a floral dress (strikingly reminiscent of the pattern on the curtain hanging over the reception window) came from an office behind the desk.

"Hello, can I help you?"

"Yeah, I've got a room booked here." He found it incredibly hard to believe that this woman was expecting more than one booking. Yet the receptionist still slowly ran her finger down the register, pushing her glasses further up the bridge of her nose whilst sucking the end of a biro pen.

"What name have you booked it under sir?" she asked not making eye contact with him but continuing to search up and down the list. Paul couldn't see the register, but he would bet that there weren't that many names on there for her to be carrying out such a strained search. He could feel his anger levels rise.

"Sergeant Paul Hargreaves."

"Let me see, hmmm. Sergeant Paul Hargreaves. Hmm…" She chewed the end of the biro, a hairline crack adding to all the others on the worn pen.

"No. I don't have a sergeant here, but I do have a Paul Hargreaves. Well, that must be you!" She looked up at Paul for the first time and looking into his eyes, there was a mischievous glint there that Hargreaves only just noticed. This old bat was loving it he thought. He was too tired to argue now, he'd put her back in her place another time. For now, all he wanted was a shower, hot food and some privacy in his own room. He made a note to himself to remember to shit in one of the cupboards before he left.

"What a pleasure it is to meet you Mr Hargreaves. DCI Chilcot has told me all about you joining our small but upstanding community. It was Charlie who booked your boarding with us himself. I'm Maggie, Welcome to the Sunyetson Inn."

It was too late to correct the hostess now. Who did this Chilcot think he was not adding his police rank to the booking? He couldn't have told her if he tried. Maggie was currently banging out a well-rehearsed script giving him details of breakfast times, dinner reservations among a mountain of other information he couldn't absorb in his current state. He continued to let her drone on until she reached behind herself to a row of hooks and removed a key with a thick brass ball as a keychain.

"Here is your key Mr Hargreaves, room four. If you follow me, I will show you the way."

Hargreaves took the key and followed the older lady up the stairs leading off from the reception area. As he closely followed her up the red carpeted staircase, he couldn't help but notice the lady's posterior. Although much older than Paul he had to admit that she had a pretty tight rump. *If I get desperate any hole and all that.* They reached the top of the stairs and headed down the corridor before stopping outside a room with the number four screwed to the door in old brass numbers. The inn probably only had around eight rooms or so he suspected. There were another five doors on this floor, a private sign hung over one which he guessed led to the attic room he saw from outside. When Hargreaves was in the lobby, he noticed a corridor leading to a couple of rooms. There hadn't been any sign of other guests, assuming there were any. Paul took the key, put it in the lock and opened the door.

"Enjoy your stay Mr Hargreaves."

Paul stepped into his room and sensed a moment of opportunity to correct her on his preferred title but as he turned back around to face Maggie, she pulled the door closed before he could spit any words out. What a bitch, so much for the farmer and his wife's opinion of Paul being in good hands, he fumed.

He found the room predictably shit. He knew the style, dark wood presumably mahogany with floral curtains, matching the bedsheets right down to the chair coverings. Paul had grown up with a mother who had a very similar taste. He couldn't care if the bed was made of fucking rosewood, it still brought back shit memories.

***

Fifteen minutes and four lines of Columbia's finest later, Paul slightly buckled at the knees as he stood over the en-suite toilet. Coaxing the last remnants of the day's tension from his manhood, Paul tossed the panties that had been clutched to his nostrils on the bathroom floor.
After struggling to have a shower in the tiny bathtub whilst the water temperature varied at a painful rate, Hargreaves dressed himself. He unpacked another designer suit from his luggage. Ordinarily Paul's wardrobe would only be the fantasy of most police sergeants, Sergeant Paul Hargreaves however was in a league of his own. He understood that within police work there were many lucrative opportunities. After dressing he picked up his hip flask from the bedroom dressing table, draining its contents. Now what he needed was food and beer, so he left the room and headed downstairs. Maggie wasn't in the reception or the little office and didn't appear regardless of Paul's constant bell ringing. He noticed that the smell of the musty fox had returned. Surveying the room Paul decided to try one of the doors off the vestibule. He found himself in a small dining room not much bigger than a modest sized living room. Maggie came through the other door holding a note pad smiling at him.

"Please take a seat Mr Hargreaves, can I get you anything to drink?"

Paul chose a table by the window and sat down.

"It's Sergeant Paul Hargreaves and yes you can get me a pint of lager. Stella if you have it. What's there to eat?"

If Maggie had heard Paul's rebuke about his name, then she didn't show it. The smile on her face never broke for a second.

"No lager I'm afraid but we do have local ale?"

Paul recoiled with disappointment, "Fuck it, just give me a bottle of whatever house red you're peddling."

"Please mind your language in the dining room Mr Hargreaves!" Maggie looked around the deserted room. Was she taking the piss or had the landlady just lost her marbles? Before he could decide Maggie continued, "Ok, one house red and we only have beef pie with all the trimmings on the menu tonight but if you would like me to whip you up a sarney instead? I'd be more than happy to oblige."

The pie sounded good to him, he was famished, and no sandwich was going to rectify that. He gave Maggie his order and she returned through the door she came in. Hargreaves looked out of the window into the garden. The sun had completely set. Having been used to the city's twenty-four-hour illumination, he couldn't believe how absolutely pitch black it was out there. He could barely make out the scarecrow which was only just visible because of the porch light's yellow glow. Maggie returned holding the bottle of corked red wine.

"Would you like to try?" she asked.

"No, I'm going to drink it either way." He had never understood this custom. Surely it was the establishment's duty to ensure the wine was of a good standard and not his. What next? The chef asking if him the beef was still in date? Maggie poured the wine and left Paul with the bottle before leaving through the serving door. Whilst he drank his wine Hargreaves thought back over the day and his evaluation of Colney so far, especially the locals. It was early days to make such an assumption, but Hargreaves didn't hold out much hope that he would ever appreciate the place. Thinking back to those he had met today he realised they had all sung the same praises for DCI Chilcot. Hargreaves didn't know what to make of that. He had been hoping for an easy ride here. He had heard things about the apparent great man but understood he was not the same hero he had once been. This Chilcot's closeness with the locals was a bit concerning, on the other hand it could mean the DCI had a weakness. Maybe this sleepy town life had softened the apparent super cop? It would make Paul's 'extracurricular activities' easier to accomplish. Maggie came back through the door with a steaming plate of food that Hargreaves had to admit smelled very good. He wouldn't tell her that though.

"Dinner is served," she laid the plate in front of him.

"Thanks, another bottle of red Maggie." He had already drained most of the first bottle. Maggie nodded and headed back to the kitchen to fetch another.

"Hang on!" she paused spinning round on her feet with a hesitant, worried look on her usually smiling face.

"Better make that two," smiled Paul with a mouthful of pie. Maggie's face instantly relaxed, her smile back.

"Of course," she headed back to the service door but just before it closed behind her, she said loud enough to be heard.

"Sergeant."

***

Hargreaves awoke with a stinging realisation of where he was, he vaguely recognised the small room through blurry eyes. The unclosed bedroom curtains told him it was now daytime. The pneumatic drill that was currently pounding into the centre of his forehead refrained for just a moment as he pulled himself up to a seated position on the side of his guestroom bed. There was a short respite until the headache came back with a new vengeance. He checked his phone that was plugged into the socket by the nightstand. At least he had done that, the clock on the display showed – 07:42 – lucky, as he clearly hadn't set an alarm. He wanted to get a lay of the land this morning before meeting up with his new superior later that day. Maybe even get a couple drinks in. The last thing he could remember from the night before in the dining room was eating his food. He had been on his way through the third or fourth bottle and recalled debating another but from there he had nothing to go on. Delicately, Hargreaves carried out his morning routine as he would anywhere else. Slash. Shit. Shower. Shave. Snort. But now he needed coffee and any bacon he could lay his hands on.

Coming down the stairs, Paul passed through the reception and went straight through the dining room door. He sat down choosing the same table as the night before. Soon enough Maggie with her smiling face came through the service entrance.

"Good morning, Mr Hargreaves," her voice far too high pitched and noisy for Paul's head this morning.

"Did you sleep okay? You certainly enjoyed the pie! You must have told me it was the best pie you tasted twenty times last night," Maggie laughed.

Did he? Paul didn't think so, it wasn't the sort of thing he'd say to a woman who had constantly infuriated him from their first encounter. His head hurt too much to disagree now though. Let her have this moment, after all he could have done a lot worse. In the past he had done a *lot* worse. He put on a forced smile and tried to laugh but it just came out as a high-pitched wheeze. Maggie's trademark smile returned indicating to Paul that his response had been enough and waited for her to take his order. But as she raised her notepad the bell from the reception rang twice.

"Oh! Excuse me for just a minute Paul, I'll be right back."

Maggie walked through to the reception just as he was about to try to correct the strange woman again, but as the door slowly swung back, he caught a glimpse of the two girls waiting out in the reception. He thought he recognised one of them, but Maggie cleared it up for him.

"Milly! Hello love. How's your mum and dad?"

The door swung closed. He held his breath as the colour drained from his face. Paul Hargreaves was a lot of things but even by his own twisted standards, even he didn't think he could sink that low. The small glimpse he had just got of the girl standing at the reception was the same girl whose underwear he had recently garnished. Ordinarily he would have enjoyed the chance encounter, that was until he saw her school uniform.

James Jenkins

LOCAL ALE

Sergeant Hargreaves walked down the picturesque street of the postcard town that he despised more than he'd feared. He scuffed his heals along the cobbled paving stones swearing as he stumbled. Quiet, beautiful towns and villages were not to Paul Hargreaves' liking, he longed for the busy streets and densely populated cities, not the close-knit communities of dreary towns long forgotten by the modern world. He studied the hanging baskets slowly rocking in the light breeze, they all had the same running theme. Communities working together to put on a show for the occasional traveller passing through or the holiday tourist. The high pollen count of the countryside was already beginning to play havoc with his sinuses, the sweet smell of flowers in bloom was a poor substitute to the thick pollution Hargreaves was used to.

Naturally, it wasn't by choice that he found himself in the Southwest of England.

He cast his mind back to the last conversation he'd had with his Bristol superior.

"It's not forever," his chief superintendent had told him.

"Just wait for the media storm to die down and we'll get you transferred back to Bristol before you know it."

Hargreaves tried to keep his rising anger back. It would do him no good to lose his cool with the super, he'd already stuck his neck out enough as it was to keep him on the force. Maybe it wouldn't be all bad.

"I hear it's a beautiful place in the summer and you will be working under DCI Chilcot," the chief said.

"Chilcot?! The super cop who lost his fucking marbles?" Hargreaves moaned.

"Watch your mouth Paul and if I were you, I'd learn some manners before you head down to Colney. True enough Chilcot took some needed time off, but I think it's hardly surprising considering the cases that man has had to work on. Kiddie fiddlers, murderers, gang related torturing you name it the man has seen and caught them all. You know you could do yourself and your career a favour by learning a thing or two from him."

Hargreaves brightened red with a mix of embarrassment and anger.

"Ok Chief but why is a big shot like him working in a sleepy town like Colney anyway? What's the current population? Ten? Do they even need a police force? Most of these sleepy towns are closing their local branches, aren't they?"

"He's had a tough life Hargreaves, is it any surprise the man would want to get away from the hard city crime? Anyway, Colney has an unusually high crime rate for such a small borough, hence the need for a local police force plus the fact that the nearest station other than its own is thirty miles away. It has a population of one thousand, one hundred and fifty-six to be precise, I suggest you learn the basics," Chief Superintendent Phipps scowled at Hargreaves.

"Must be a lot of chicken rustling cases then," Hargreaves smirked.

"Get your stuff packed and get out of here Sergeant, you're lucky you still have somewhere to go. There's not a whole deal of takers for you and DCI Chilcot is sticking his neck out to do me a favour here. Now get going, keep your head down and maybe if you behave yourself, we'll consider getting you a transfer later. For now, get the fuck out of my office!"

The whole incident had left a bad taste in his mouth. Sure, he bent the rules at times, but it was all for the greater good. Hargreaves got his job done and got his man. Most of the time. What did it matter if he made a little profit now and then?

A pretty lady smiled his way as she come out of the little village store that he considered lucky to have not been changed into a Tesco. Paul returned the smile although it would have appeared a dirty sneer at best. She dipped her head and turned away walking up the street away from him. "Stuck up cow," he muttered. Still at least with a bit of gear like that walking about it showed there might be a chance to wet his wick yet. Especially now young Millie was off limits, for the time being at least. Hell, there weren't many whores left in Bristol that Hargreaves hadn't screwed, at least he'd temporarily satisfied his urges before leaving. Hargreaves stopped by a thatched cottage where an elderly man was setting up a scarecrow in his front garden. Hargreaves had seen more and more of them today after leaving the guest house. The landlady Maggie had explained that the annual scarecrow festival was one of the community's favourite events after he had finished his breakfast that morning. Fucking inbred idiots need to get out more.

He spotted an elderly man watering some flowers outside a shop and caught his attention.

"Where can I find the Ivy Tavern?" Hargreaves said with his air of arrogant authority.

"Yes, dear boy, carry on straight the way you are heading and turn left at the church. The Ivy is just behind it," the friendly villager replied.

"Cheers," said Hargreaves before turning on his heal.

"Hold up, you're not from round here are you dear boy? You wouldn't be…"

But Hargreaves had already picked up his pace leaving the local staring at the back of his head. He had no intention of making small talk with these backward green fingered farmers.

Sergeant Hargreaves arrived at the Ivy Tavern. The country pub with its thatched roof and thick ivy exterior would have pleased most people. Not Hargreaves, he much preferred the generic, well known pub chain that lacked any soul. Paul walked into the bristling pub leaving the late spring sunshine outside. He was slightly surprised to only observe the odd punter turn around to see who had stepped into their local. The bar was well kept and clean, not what he expected to see at all. They even had Stella on tap. Paul walked up to the bar with a cocksure swagger.

"What can I get you sir?" asked a kindly looking gentleman who was drying a pint glass with a dish cloth.

"Pint of Stella," Hargreaves answered as if it was a demand and not a request. The barkeep's demeanour changed somewhat from a cheery fellow to that of someone who had been slapped in the face before changing to a slightly pitying look.

"Stella's off tap at the moment I'm afraid sir. Maybe you would like to try one of our local ales instead?"

Paul winced casting his eye over the oddly named pumps that he was sure contained some watery pretentious piss that wasn't even carbonated.

"Whatever, just nothing too dark..." Hargreaves grumbled. "You wouldn't find pubs in the city running out of lager mate."

The bar tender started to pour Hargreaves' pint from a pump with a caricature of a dead sheep upturned on its back with crosses for eyes. The ale was named 'Sheep's Misfortune'. Sheep's piss more like thought the sergeant.

"You're a long way from the city here friend," the bar keeper replied without catching Paul's eye.

"Believe me I didn't choose to be in this backward little shit hole, why anyone in their right fucking mind would come to this scarecrow worshipping Wicker Man inspired land that time forgot I don't know."

The bar keeper shook his head and tutted. He put down the glass he had been filling.

"I'm going to have to ask you to watch your mouth sir, this is a family pub attended by our community so if you don't like it, please feel free to go back out of the door you came from. That is after you pay for your drink."

Paul laughed, "I'm not paying for that glass of farmer's piss mate. You can stick your ale up your arse!"

"Then I will have to call the police if you can't calm yourself down," The bar keeper threatened, visibly flustered.

Paul grabbed his badge from his suit jacket. Yet another costly purchase. He thrust the identification within inches of the bar keeper's angered face.

"I'll save you the trouble pal! Sergeant Paul Hargreaves, Colney's newest member of the police force. I see I'm going to have to keep an eye on you… What is your name anyway?"

A hand from behind weighted down on Paul's shoulder expertly squeezing his muscle to make him wince, he spun around to face the perpetrator ready to take physical action if required.

"I suggest you calm down, pay for your drink and apologise to Harry here. Harry's family have run this pub for three generations, and I can assure you he has the love and support of this whole community. You, young man, seem to be causing quite the scene with your rude, aggressive approach and as you can see the whole pub is finding it quite the show." True enough, Paul scanned the faces of everyone in the pub, all frozen in shock and anticipating his next response.

Hargreaves turned back to face the man who seemed to stare at Paul with such intensity he may have been looking into his soul. The older bloke was big, not just tall but built up all over his gargantuan frame. He wasn't what you'd call fat but what Hargreaves would describe as hench. The sergeant who was no short arse himself, noticed something about the man. A quiet air of confidence accompanied the physical presence of him. Paul would have to put this interfering punter in his place, nip it in the bud right away.

"You just insulted an officer of the law pal."

"Your career as an officer of the law greatly hinges upon my say so by the way I see it, so now is the time to put that badge back in your pocket and find some manners," the man said with a calm un- obnoxious sense of authority.

"Who the fuc…" Paul was cut off from his foul-mouthed response as the same pretty lady he had seen earlier came rushing through the tavern door.

"DCI Chilcot!" the woman half shouted half panted, "It's gone! Someone has stolen the church scarecrow!"

Paul's mouth fell open.

"Ok Helen. Thank you for letting me know. I will come and have a look later after I've… inducted my new sergeant in the social decorum around here, see if you can get hold of Fred for now," DCI Chilcot replied whilst never taking his eyes away from Paul's. Helen nodded at Harry and a couple of other shocked customers. After Helen left, the other punters in the pub resumed their former conversations, turning their attention away from the confrontation at the bar.

"Sir I'm truly sorry," Paul whined, offering his hand to the superior officer.

"Let's start again shall we Sergeant Hargreaves?" Chilcot suggested.

"Thanks Guv, sorry, it's just been a bad few days." Paul reddened dropping any of his obstinate attitude.

"Not settling in then boy? Colney is a beautiful place and if given the respect they so deserve so are the residents. Now your Chief Superintendent Phipps and I go way back and although I don't know the extent of your current demotion, I can assure you that it's only out of respect to Phipps that I have thrown you this lifeline. Pick your pint up and join me Hargreaves. As you just witnessed yourself there has been a crime committed so let's get the introductions done so we can start doing some policework!" Chilcot said before turning to the bar keeper, "Put his drinks on my tab Harry."

As Hargreaves followed his new boss away from the bar, he could have sworn he heard the bar keeper say to another punter,

"Another Stella Sam?"

Both officers settled down in a snug by the corner of the bar.

"Excuse me Guv," Paul started, "I don't want to be rude or come across unappreciative of you extending the olive branch here, but I just don't see the need for much policework in a small place like this. You said it yourself, this is a close-knit community so surely there isn't much crime. Barring the case of the missing scarecrow that is! I'm just used to bigger things."

"A crime is a crime, Sergeant. Also, as I've learnt over the years some things aren't always as innocent as they seem. A small crime that lies closer to the scales of justice is much easier to go to sleep with than those of a more monstrous nature. A good officer should be happy that no crimes are ever committed rather than lusting for crimes of a more serious nature just to help promote their own career," DCI Chilcot scorned.

"I get your point, Sir, but surely all that training I received wasn't just for a bit of illegal scrumpy making or a bit of farmer/chicken sexual relations," prattled Hargreaves, smirking at his own reply.

"Perhaps I should enlighten you, Sergeant? Colney, as I am sure you have already been informed, has an unusually high crime rate for the ratio of residents that live here. We also police the local district including neighbouring towns and villages such as Hurnsey and Turnstone. Most of these cases are, as you have so obnoxiously pointed out, relatively low priority incidents. However, few other cases have been as distressing, sinister and strange as you would ever need to hear in your whole life let alone police career."

"Ok, you've got me intrigued Guv. I don't suppose in any of these stories it transpires there's a knocking shop round here though is there?" Hargreaves purred with a glazed look in his eye, his arrogance beginning to rise to the surface again as he tested his new Boss.

"No Sergeant Hargreaves. As I said, I won't pretend to know the reasons for your transfer but what I do know about you, encourages me to advise you to put that part of you behind for now. Now, do you want to hear about Colney's darker side of the law and thus gain a greater understanding of this community? Or shall I send you back to Bristol and your former vices?"

Parochial Pigs

"Nothing I've ever done wrong Guv. The papers and these rent a gobs are always trying to smear us good officers, I just want to do my bit here and wait for the media storm to calm down then I'll be out of your hair and back in Brizzle before you know it. My record speaks for itself; I always get my man...mostly," Paul piped up forgetting himself once again.

"Your record certainly looks good on paper Sergeant but what methods were used I wonder. What murky cover ups could a good reporter find if they wanted to? Imagine what another police officer could find out about your 'methods' and at what price did these cost others innocent or not? This is your last chance saloon and I am your maker. I have no interest in releasing a bent cop back into the city's underworlds, so I suggest you knuckle down here Hargreaves, or you will be attending Colney's scarecrow festivals for many more years to come," DCI Chilcot seethed.

"You're right Boss. Sorry, please fill me in. If you help me get out of these backwaters, I'll promise to crack on and do an honest job," Paul lied with some conviction. So what if he told DCI tosspot what he wanted to hear, all that mattered was getting out of here and getting back to business in the city. Policework was about so much more than just keeping the peace and catching criminals.

James Jenkins

THE CASE OF THE EXTRA SUITCASE

"Well then, let me begin!" DCI Chilcot said, "This first case happened a short time after I arrived here from the city myself. I was asked to investigate a missing woman from the community by a worried neighbour. The missing woman was married to a well-known resident of the town. Dennis Carter. Naturally when a married woman goes missing and is only reported by her neighbour and not her husband alarm bells really do start ringing. The concerned neighbour Mrs Wells knew the Carter's well enough. She and Mrs Carter attended church events together and both held seats on the local primary school's board of committee. One morning Mrs Wells was walking round to the Carter's house when she saw Dennis unloading a rather large suitcase from the boot of his car. 'Hello Dennis. Is Margaret home at all?'. 'No, I'm afraid she's gone to stay with her sister in Rhossili Bay. I dropped her off at the station earlier this morning Diane,' Dennis replied whilst closing the boot of his car. 'Oh? She never told me she was off,' said Diane Wells. 'Last minute I'm afraid as her sister has come down quite unwell and as Margaret is her only living relative, she has gone to look after her for a few weeks. They were always very close after they lost their mother a few years back.' Diane nodded with a look of sympathy. 'Yes, I remember Margaret telling me about it before. Poor girls. Well, I wish her sister a speedy recovery. I guess she overpacked then?' Diane said with a chuckle. Dennis looked slightly puzzled, 'Sorry?' he replied. 'The suitcase Dennis!' Dennis looked down at the heavy suitcase that he'd struggled to lift out of the boot."

Parochial Pigs

"He killed his wife and stuck her in the suitcase! Pretty twisted but it's hardly human trafficking or a gang related drive-by, is it?" Sergeant Hargreaves butted in.

"How very perceptive of you. But perhaps not everything is always as it seems Hargreaves. If you'd let me finish?"

Hargreaves stopped talking and took another mouthful of beer letting the chief continue.

"Dennis Carter stared nervously at the suitcase. It was as if he didn't realise he'd been holding it, let alone seen it before. 'The suitcase… Yes, Margaret forgot to take it out of the boot.' Mrs Wells eyed Mr Carter with an air of suspicion. 'How will she ever get on without her clothes?' she cried. 'Well, urm. I've already called her mobile to let her know. She said it's a good excuse to go on a shopping trip,' Carter said a little too quickly. 'Shopping trip in a remote place like Worms Head! Ha! She'll be lucky!' Mrs Wells laughed. 'Okay, I'll be seeing you Dennis and don't forget I will be round later in the week to inspect your scarecrow for the annual scarecrow event. I notice you haven't got it up yet but I'm sure we can rely on the Carter's to keep up with tradition. I do hope Margaret is back in time to sit on the judge panel with me at the end of the month.'
Diane walked back down the garden path leaving Mr Carter to drag the suitcase into his house. As Diane closed the little wrought iron gate, she looked back up the path to where Mr Carter still struggled with the case. Diane could have sworn that she saw something inside move. Mr Carter saw her looking, he quickly pressed his knee into the side of the suitcase straining a smile. 'See you later Diane,' he said and turned his back on her."

"So, the neighbour reports it, you go around there and find his wife's body stuffed into the bed springs of his mattress or something?"

"That certainly would have been the straightforward scenario, Sergeant, but as I already told you. Each one of these cases are strangely unique and even though you paint a pretty picture of the missing wife it is still perhaps more stomach-able than the reality."

"What?! Alright you've got me hooked. Please go on." Hargreaves settled back into the soft cushioning of the pub furniture.

DCI Chilcot laughed, "Oh, I've got you hooked alright! Need another drink, Paul? More Farmer's piss I'm afraid though." Chilcot got up from the table and walked the short distance to the bar where Harry had already placed two fresh pints of beer.

"It's not as bad as I first thought actually Guv. Yeah, another pint please," Hargreaves called out to his new boss.

It was true, much to his surprise he was enjoying the cloudy flat alcohol more than ever he realised was possible. Paul drained the last dregs of his glass. Must be quite pokey too he thought. He could already feel the happy buzz that mildly numbed the soul after four or five Stellas. Shit, he hadn't even thought about nipping to the shithouse for a cheeky whiff either. At least not yet. DCI Chilcot sat back down at their table placing Paul's pint in front him.

"Cheers Sergeant."

"Cheers Guv. Next rounds on me." Hargreaves raised his glass.

Parochial Pigs

"You're new here Paul. Think of it as a welcoming drink. Anyway, where was I?" DCI Chilcot sat back down across from his sergeant.

"Ah yes. So, Mrs Wells didn't actually raise her suspicions to our good selves until a few days later."

"What?! Why not?"

"You must remember Sergeant; people are very close around here. It takes quite a lot for people to begin seeing the worse in their neighbours. Neighbours who were perhaps once school friends, members of the community who teach their children, doctors and nurses. It takes a lot for people to see the worst in each other. Although you do seem to be an exception to the rule from what I've heard about your short time in Colney already."

What did he mean by that? Paul wondered. Probably that loopy cow Maggie snitching on him. Hargreaves felt that he had given her just the amount of respect that was deserved after the mind games. Having said that, there was still some unaccounted-for memories between that third bottle of wine and waking up in his room this morning. The DCI swallowed a mouthful of his drink and continued.

"So, Mrs Carter's absence from our charming community wasn't reported to the police until a few days later after Mrs Wells returned to the Carter's household to inspect Mr Carter's scarecrow. When Mrs Wells arrived at the Carter house and walked up the garden path, she noticed two things amiss. One was the lack of any scarecrow.
Now, Mrs Wells takes her position in the town very seriously and sees any lack of effort by other residents, a personal attack on her own reputation. So naturally when she also

noticed the front door standing wide open, she threw concern for her friend's wellbeing out of her mind and marched straight through the open door into the Carter house and straight into the large farmhouse kitchen. 'Dennis! Dennis! Why is your scarecrow still not up? The festival starts tomorrow.' She stopped in her tracks as the door leading to the kitchen's large walk-in pantry flew open. Mr Carter slipped in, looking flushed as beads of sweat ran off his brow. He covered the opening of the door with his body before slamming it closed. Carter stood there looking like a wild man, eyes bloodshot, nostrils damp with bodily fluids either from tears or exertion. He was naked from the waist up and appeared to have scratches or cuts on his upper torso. 'GET OUT OF HERE DIANE! GET OUT FUCKING NOW!!!' he raged with spittle flying out of his cracked and chapped lips. 'I'm sssorry Dennis, I just saw there was no scarecrow in the...' she stammered. 'GET OUT AND FUCK YOUR FUCKING SCARECROW YOU INTERFERING OLD COW GO!!!'

Now naturally Mrs Wells took Mr Carter's advice and flew out of that house, down the garden path and out through the gate quicker than an attorney threatened with feticide. This is when I first met dear Mrs Wells. Diane made her statement divulging her two previous visits to the Carter house as well as mentioning that although Mrs Carter was not unknown to visit her sister up to three or four times a year, she always let Mrs Wells, or another member of the school board know before doing so. I must admit although the story did seem out of the ordinary, I didn't know the town's people very well at the time and wondered if Mrs Wells was perhaps exaggerating. I mean I'm not entirely sure how I would feel if someone just walked into my house without my knowing."

Hargreaves chuckled before chiming in, "If it weren't for the suitcase stuff, I'd think she had just walked in on him with Rosey Palmer and her five sisters!"

"As crude as your choice of language is Hargreaves I briefly came to the same conclusion after we checked Margaret Carter's whereabouts. But first I went to see Mr Carter at his house."

"Now Mr Carter didn't grow up in Colney. He married his wife after they met at university. He was always a city slicker and only moved here because Mrs Carter pleaded with him to move back to her childhood town. Dennis was polite enough but the feeling in the village was he didn't like to be here. I asked him about his wife's whereabouts to which he replied with the same story as he told Mrs Wells. We talked about his visit from Mrs Wells and he told me she had taken him by surprise especially as he was half dressed. He made sure to point this out to me that this was his right in his own home and even asked what we would be doing concerning Mrs Wells trespassing on his property. All in all, I could sense quite a defensive man in Mr Carter. So, I asked him 'Mr Carter, Mrs Wells said that you seemed to come out of the pantry. I hope it's not too strange a question, but can I ask what you were doing in there that would cause you to be so alarmed at the time Mrs Wells called by?'

'I'm afraid I won't be able to answer that question, Officer. I can't let you look inside it without a warrant either as I'm sure you were about to ask me. I don't want to seem like I am being awkward. The truth is I am embarrassed about what is behind that door, but it is nothing to do with my wife being on holiday nor is it anything that authorities need concern themselves with. My wife will be back next week, and you will see that for yourself Officer. Anything in the meantime will require a warrant I'm afraid. Now if you don't mind,' Dennis droned. 'Maybe you could provide us with an address or phone number we can contact Mrs Carter at?' I asked. 'I'm afraid it would do you no good. Margaret left her phone in the car when I left her at the station,' Carter said."

"I thought he told Mrs Wells he called his wife about the suitcase!?" Hargreaves interrupted.

"Exactly Sergeant. I'm glad you're still with us. Hang on let me get Harry to bring us another drink over... Harry. Can we get the same again please?"

Hargreaves was on the edge of his seat. His adrenaline was making him shiver anxiously awaiting the next part of the super's story. Maybe it's the lack of marching powder he'd had today. Still the beer at least seemed to be having a good effect on him.

"So," Chilcot continued, "I asked him, 'Mrs Wells said you had phoned your wife to tell her about the suitcase Mr Carter. How would you have been able to call your wife if she indeed had no phone?' His response was just that he had simply said it to get Mrs Wells to go away and stop bothering him about scarecrows. I was deeply suspicious but not sure if we had enough to get a search warrant on him yet, but I do have a friend in Rhossili Bay and thought I could probably find out if Mrs Carter had a sister there. 'Well thanks for your time, Mr Carter and if you do hear from your wife any earlier, please do not hesitate to get in contact with us.' Dennis saw me out of his front door, 'Goodbye Officer.' He watched me as I came to that wrought iron gate that Mrs Wells had made a beeline for only days ago. 'Oh! One more thing Mr Carter. Do you still have the suitcase packed with your wife's belongings?' I asked. 'No officer, I'm afraid I don't remember what I did with it.' Poppy cock I thought. 'You must admit Mr Carter this all does look very suspicious, as is your failure to comply,' I said. 'Officer my wife is neither dead nor is she missing. If you were to obtain a search warrant and later my wife returns collaborating my story, then the whole situation could leave you in a rather unfortunate mess. I have my own high placed friends in the force as you know. So, I would advise you wait until my wife gets home and forget about this storm in a teacup until then'. I couldn't work out what he was playing at, all I could do was wait for my contact in Rhossili Bay to see if he could track Mrs Carter down or wait for her to come home. My other worry was Mr Carter doing a runner and just delaying us for time. A couple days later we were investigating another case in the town where what looked like a group of youngsters had been camping in the woodlands. There was a burnout car in the clearing where the tents were, and the nearby farmer was missing a couple of his livestock."

Hargreaves rolled his eyes. "Wow! I was wrong. A bunch of kids, A burned out car and a couple of fucking sheep! Haha."

DCI Chilcot shot Hargreaves with a stare. "That was still someone's car Hargreaves, that farmer lost money on those animals and please try and watch your language… Anyway. Constable Hirst came over to give me a message that had been sent from Mrs Carter! Apparently, Mr Carter had gone all out to contact her after my visit. I went back to the station straight away leaving the car and livestock to the constable and PCO, so that I could call her back. She confirmed that what Mr Carter told me had been true about her sickly sister and the suddenness of her having to leave. She even gave us the details of the hospital her sister had been admitted too, so we could verify the story. It all checked out. Margaret said her sister was now settling back home and she herself would be returning in a couple of days. So that was it, no missing person, no case."

Hargreaves shrugged his shoulders, not hiding his disappointment, "So, what you're saying is one of the biggest crimes committed here wasn't even a crime but some old busy body getting her facts wrong because she's so desperate for some entertainment in her dull and unfulfilling life?"

"No Sergeant. One of the biggest and weirdest crimes that happened in this town was exposed only because of the old busy body getting her facts wrong."

"What are you on about Guv? Isn't that it or did you get to see his porn collection?"

"As I said earlier, I came to that conclusion too. I mean he didn't just have an alibi but no victim. He was off the hook. That was until Mrs Carter came home.
Mrs Carter had caught a taxi back from the station so as not to bother her husband with having to wait for a train to come in at the right time, especially seeing as she didn't have her mobile phone to let him know. The taxi driver said in his statement, 'Margaret was very excited about surprising Dennis.' Well, it was Margaret Carter who was in for the surprise. Dennis was nowhere to be seen. Margaret searched the house finding her mobile phone on the living room table. She plugged it in and tried Dennis' number. The phone rang out, but no one answered. His car was in the driveway so Mrs Carter assumed although wishfully, that he may have ventured

out into the town making friends with the locals. Whilst waiting for her husband, Mrs Carter remembered that she'd promised to call me when she got home. Just to clarify everything regarding her missing person report. I answered my phone, 'DCI Chilcot. How can I help?'. 'Hello Officer, its Margaret Carter here, you said I should give you a call when I got back.' I was over on Donovan McKay's farm at the time. He was the farmer who'd had his livestock stolen and more had been going missing that week. 'Hi, yes thank you for calling me back, Margaret. When's convenient for you?' I'd completely forgotten about it to be honest as we knew Mrs Carter had confirmed her whereabouts. She said, 'Now is ok if it is with you? Also, I know this sounds strange, but I haven't seen Dennis since I've been back, and it's been nearly four hours now. He's not much of a drinker and is a bit shy with the community so I don't think he would be at the Ivy or anything.' I snapped at the chance. I assumed Mr Carter's whereabouts were not suspicious and that he would turn up soon, but I couldn't wait to get a look inside that so-called pantry. So, I told Mrs Carter I would be round straight away. When I got there, we sat at the same table her husband and I had only days ago and after she'd confirmed her whereabouts again, I noticed Mrs Carter's suitcases at the front door. 'That's a lot of luggage Mrs Carter. I take it you didn't miss anything?' Blushing slightly, she responded 'Well you know what they say about women and their clothes Mr Chilcot.' I asked Mrs Carter when she had last phoned her husband, 'I tried him again just before you arrived.' She said her phone was still plugged in inside the living room and went to get it.

While she left, I started to think about a tactful way of getting a peak in the pantry door, if Mr Carter was hiding something from Mrs Carter, I would need to be very careful so as not to cause Margaret any unnecessary upset. Most of the time with these little pervs it's just a bit of spanking or BDSM stuff. A secret to keep away from the Mrs, but there's always the worry they are harbouring much darker things. However, I must confess that my curiosity was beginning to get the better of me and who knew if Mr Carter would come through that door at any minute putting an end to my chances of an unwarranted search. 'Mrs Carter?' I said as she walked back into the kitchen with her mobile phone, I think she had just pressed redial. 'Would you mind if I just had a look inside your...' There it was! That deep frequency vibration of a mobile phone. Very slight but I could hear it and so could she, now she wasn't calling as far away as the living room. 'Where is it?' she said. 'It's coming from the pantry, let me look. Stand back please Mrs Carter...' I opened the door to the pantry and caught a terrible stench of mould and meat. The pantry was a pantry sure enough, but I could hear the phone vibrating below me. 'Do you think he's in the cellar?' asked Maggie Carter. 'Cellar? I thought this was a pantry,' I said. Sure, enough I looked down to where the trap door was. Still with me Sergeant?"

"Yes Guv!" Paul's delayed response snapped out of his slack jawed mouth; he was enjoying himself much to his surprise, hanging on to his superior's every word. The old super-cop wasn't so bad. A bit of a stickler to the rules by the sounds of it, but Hargreaves had no doubt in his mind he could get him around his little finger after a few weeks. Plus, he had to admit the beer was really helping. "What happened next?"

"I opened the hatch and the stench that swept up my nostrils hit me like a roundhouse. Decaying meat mixed with the faint smell of bad seafood and bleach. I walked down the

Parochial Pigs

steps and found a door at the bottom. It was a reinforced slab of metal, I don't know the technical stuff, but it's meant to keep rooms airtight; a sort of walk-in fridge found in large restaurant kitchens I suppose would be a fair comparison. How the hell he got someone to fit it down there still escapes me. Anyway, the door's slightly ajar and as I try to open it something gets in the way grunting as I force myself through the opening... A pig! I kid you not Sergeant Hargreaves."

"A fucking pig in the basement!" Hargreaves exploded with enjoyment, "I was so right about this town."

"Quite. Well it was at this point I realised we had a potential bestiality case on our hands, so I naturally called for backup and advised Mrs Carter to go and stay with her neighbour, a close friend. Whilst waiting, I decided to investigate further and after going through the door into the cellar of which can only be described as a BDSM slaughterhouse for livestock I was sick for the first time since seeing my first dead body. Carter laid on the floor, where the man's genitals had once been was now a ragged hole of flesh and exposed pink tissue bled out onto the cellar floor. A congealed and sticky puddle surrounded the husband's body. The pig I had seen earlier was eating at the flesh around the wound as he lay there dead. For reasons my mind will never fully comprehend the pig was wearing leather bondage style clothing and as I looked around this hellish place, I saw that the room was adorned with home developed photos of every farm animal you could imagine, all dressed in a similar fashion to the pig. Some of the images included Mr Carter himself. A camera and tripod in the corner of the rank smelling room indicated that a third party wasn't involved. I had seen more than enough; I moved to Colney for a quiet life yet here I stood two months in and surrounded in blood, pig shit and semen. Still, it did help me solve the missing livestock case. Like I said Sergeant, not every case is as simple as it seems."

"Bloody Hell Guv, that's fucking sick! What did his Mrs make of it all?"

"She grieved but she's a strong woman Maggie and she moved on. She even got her *scarecrow* up that year! As Maggie does every year. Maybe it helped."

"What? She still lives here?" Hargreaves had still failed to make the link.

"Yes of course. Why, I believe you've already had the pleasure of meeting her? Seeing as she's your landlady?"

"What? She failed to mention any of that. Bloody hell I knew something wasn't right about that place." Hargreaves grimaced remembering the smell coming from the taxidermy fox.

"Fear not Sergeant, Mrs Carter sold the house after that. Too many memories I suppose. Plus, after the heartache of losing her husband and learning of his past it was perhaps too much to share with a stranger."

"Did they ever find the suitcase?"

"That's the funny thing. With the worry of her husband being missing, Maggie had forgot about the suitcase. When I mentioned her extra luggage at the house it clearly hadn't registered important enough for her to remember at the time. She had packed it with several of her mother's belongings that she wanted to take to her sister. We found it after searching

Parochial Pigs

the house and it all checked out. The irony is if Maggie hadn't forgot the suitcase, then I dare say we would have never suspected Mr Carter in the first place."

Hargreaves took it all in. The old boy could spin a yarn alright, well, if he was buying the beers who cares. This seemed like a good time to empty his bladder.

"Where's the gents in hear Guv?"

Chilcot pointed towards the left-hand side of the bar as Hargreaves struggled to his feet. The hair of the dog had certainly cleared his earlier headache but now the ale mixed with last night's wine was taking its toll upon him. The tipsy sergeant concentrated his footsteps and headed for the restroom door marked with a picture of a male scarecrow with an eerie smile, he checked the ladies room door which also had a scarecrow picture, this one wearing a dress and a bonnet on its head. "They're a simple bunch this lot," Hargreaves mused to himself. He pushed open the door to the smell of piss and urinal cakes in the air. After fumbling with his fly to release his manhood, he let out a sigh of relief as the deeply yellow liquid hit the porcelain bowl. His eyes scanned around to locate the toilet cubicle which was shut and had a handwritten out-of-order sign cello-taped to the door. Pity he thought, but perhaps it was a good thing. If this Chilcot was the copper everyone said he was then Hargreaves didn't want to risk being found out on his first day. The booze was doing ok, for now at least, keeping his itch scratched, wasn't it? – maybe just a quick one? Before squirting out the last of his bladder, Hargreaves made sure to add a puddle on the toilet floor. A bit of payback for Harry the barkeeper's lip earlier. A small victory, but one he still took a slice of pleasure from. Hargreaves tucked himself back in and headed to the wash hand basins, the grime covered surface would have to suffice as he poured out a conservative amount of the drug. Covering one nostril with his hand he inhaled deeply and swung his head up as the toilet door swung open. Shit! The face of a stranger quickly looked away and walked over to the urinal. Too close, he thought, but the risk just added to the high.

Vacating the toilets, he willed his wobbly legs back over to the waiting DCI, who was now talking with two other police officers. One with the stripes of a police constable and the other a widely frowned upon PCO. Hargreaves moved his mildly groggy head towards the pair as he slid back into his seat with the grace of a new-born calf. The three men paused their conversation.

"Good afternoon," chirped the constable in a strong West Country accent.

"Who's your friend Chief?" enquired the PCO in an equally laughable accent to Hargreaves.

Hargreaves cast a critical eye over the pair, who to him resembled something like an eighty's comedy duo. The PCO was considerably shorter with stumpy legs than his immediate superior, with a balding crown and the start of a beer belly. Fucking hobby bobby Hargreaves chimed to himself. At least the constable looked like he would be capable of chasing a criminal Hargreaves observed. He was holding a bouquet of flowers. The constable grinned at him with a face that Hargreaves strongly suspected had all the makings of years of inbreeding. The pair looked exactly as he would have expected from two small-town inferior officers.

"Meet Sergeant Paul Hargreaves," Chilcot said with a slight emphasis of enjoyment.

"Nice to meet you, Paul! I guess we will be working closely together from now on," the constable beamed.

"That's Sergeant Hargreaves to you," Hargreaves smugly retorted.

"Oh, I think we can leave out the formalities today, Paul. After all you don't officially start until tomorrow, so you could say for the time being Fred and Martin are your superiors," Chilcot laughed.

"No offense meant Sergeant." said the constable who Chilcot had pointed out as Fred.

"None whatsoever from me neither Guv," Martin the PCO offered.

Hargreaves privately praised himself for stamping his authority over these two. Got to let them know who's the boss early on Pauly boy he told himself. He grinned at the two men.

"Ok boys. No problem really, as long as we all understand the chain of command then we should all get on just fine!" he mused.

"Quite," said Chilcot giving Paul what could have been a look to remind him the same thing.

"I've just been telling Pau... Sorry my mistake, Sergeant Hargreaves," Chilcot corrected himself. Paul didn't think the DCI had made the mistake by accident.

Chilcot continued, "I've been telling the sergeant about some of the history of Colney and the district constabulary's past cases. In fact, I'm sure you boys will probably have a story or two yourselves?"

"Oh yes Chief!" said Fred.

"Let me tell him about the Packman boys over in Hurnsey!" joined in Martin rather excitedly.

Look at them! Hargreaves thought. They are like a couple of green schoolboys. He'd have these two singing to his tune in no time.

"No! Not that one, that's weird that is. Let's tell him about the 'Postcard Killer' from Turnstone!" said Fred.

Chilcot smiled at the two officers like a parent would to two overly excited children.

"You boys can tell Paul here whatever case you fancy but just don't go telling him about Alice. Leave that one for me if you will." The Chief stood up from his chair and taking it from the back of his seat, begun to put on his coat.

"Where are you off to Chief?" asked Martin with a look of worry, perhaps from being left alone with the less than friendly new police sergeant.

"I just need to check in on my wife lad's. I promised her," Chilcot replied.

"Oh... Okay Guv. Here's the flowers you asked me to pick up from Mrs Pettigrew's store," said Fred handing over the large bouquet of white lilies. Hargreaves thought the constable had a slight look of something like embarrassment about him as he passed them over to the chief. Paul also noticed the chief had a sad look in his eyes as he received the flowers.

"I won't be long Sergeant. I apologise for leaving you, but I promise you would be hard pushed to find better company in the whole of Colney than that of Police Constable Fred Hirst and Community Officer Martin Spettigue. Keep it to the book boys, I don't want any unnecessary adornment in your tails." And with that Chilcot headed for the tavern door turning back to the bar just before leaving.

"Harry, drinks are on me for my officers. Just watch Martin." He winked at the PCO "Don't forget boys, you are still on duty." Chilcot turned and left through the door into the late afternoon sunshine.

This might work out alright. A little time with these two dumb witted twats and Hargreaves might get a better picture regarding the DCI. It would also give him a suitable opportunity to establish authority over the two lower ranked officers and without the chief sticking up for them. It was clear that the DCI thought highly of the pair. DCI Chilcot had looked at them as if they were a couple of pet labradors rather than that of professional law and order workers.

Hargreaves changed his body language instantly.

"So, how did two highly intelligent individuals as yourselves end up in such a shithole as this?" he leered.

"Thank you for noticing Sergeant although I do take offense to you calling Colney a shithole," said Martin not sensing Hargreaves' sarcasm.

"You see." joined in Fred, "Both Martin and I were brought up right here in Colney."

Hargreaves laughed, "You poor fuckers!"

"Well where did you grow up then Mr Bigshot?!" Martin almost stammered.

"Don't take it to heart Martin, city slickers like our new sergeant here don't always appreciate the country life we have been privileged to. He is welcome to his own opinion as are we. Maybe Sergeant Hargreaves will adjust to life here after some time and it's not like Colney and our neighbouring towns and villages don't have enough exciting police files to explore," calmed Fred.

"From what I hear the sergeant won't be around long enough for that," Martin smirked gleefully.

"Enough Martin! That's none of your business and you know it," Fred warned.

Phew thought Hargreaves. At least they didn't expect him to stick around here too long. The DCI must have told the other officers he would be transferred back to Bristol soon. That reassured him.

"It's ok Martin. You are right, I'm not planning on staying here too long. Just enough time for the press to forget about me and I'll be out of your *Hot Fuzz* for good. Now, I believe you boys had a story to tell. The chief already filled me in on historical pig fucking and your annual scarecrow drivel so anything with a bit less bestiality wouldn't go a miss!" the sergeant said finishing his beer.

"Let me grab a round," said Martin as he headed to the bar.

Too right thought Hargreaves. The alcohol was the only thing that would make anything these two soft wankers said any fun.

Fred pulled up another chair presumably for Martin and sat himself down into the chief's chair.

"Okay Sergeant Hargreaves let's see what you make of this one," he chuckled.

James Jenkins

LITTLE BOXES

Fred cleared his throat and began his tale, "DCI Chilcot sent Martin and me over to Turnstone a couple years back. Like Hurnsey and Abergreen, Turnstone is under the Colney Police Constabulary. It's only a twenty-minute drive from here down near the coast, so it was no surprise to investigate a suspected container washing up on the beach. You see Sergeant, it really is not uncommon. As you can imagine containers that fall off container ships draw in a big crowd of scavengers. Sometimes the containers contain high-end goods, some of which can be salvaged before the salty water has caused any lasting damage to the goods."

Martin returned to the table struggling to hold the three pints of lager. As Martin sloppily passed the glasses out and took the vacant seat, Hargreaves reflected on this potential opportunity. After all, some of those containers were bound to contain drugs or other illegal items and if he was ever called to the scene, it might be possible to skim some off the top for his – *Christmas Bonus* – as he liked to call such perversions of the law.

"Cheers Martin," said Fred.

"Err, yeah," said Hargreaves distractedly.

He noticed the other two officer's glasses contained a much lighter ale than his own. Pansies, he thought. They'd obviously taken the chief's warning about not drinking too much quite literally.

"Are you telling him about the Packman boys Fred?" Martin said between sipping his over spilling pint.

"No Martin, It's not appropriate. Plus, I'm sure our new sergeant here will find this story even more entertaining," Fred continued, "Like I was saying. Some of these containers contain high end goods such as cars, designer clothing, agricultural equipment even smuggled goods such as drugs."

Sergeant Paul Hargreaves suppressed a grin.

"Now as local law enforcement we don't usually get that close to the goods. That's down to the custom boys and the coastguard are usually the first to arrive. We are just there to keep the hoards at bay so to speak."

Bollocks! thought Hargreaves.

"However, it is not all together unusual for us to be first on the scene as we were on this occasion and it doesn't hurt to have a quick sneak peek," relayed Fred.

Get in! thought Hargreaves.

"Not for our own benefit mind," Fred quickly added "but it helps to know if there is anything hazardous inside, I'm sure you understand, risk assessments being mandatory these days. But on this occasion, there was nothing more interesting than your standard flat screen televisions, blu ray players and other electrical household goods. Certainly nothing worth salvaging after the elements had gotten to it, which made Martin's and my job all the easier to deter would-be treasure hunters. At least most of them. You see Sergeant, the container was reported to us by a local fisherman called Ian Steiner who warned us there were already a few people on the scene who had taken their chances with the goods, loading what they could and making a sharp exit before we arrived. Fortunately for us, our law-abiding fisherman had taken note of one of the registration plates of a grey Citroen Berlingo van that had been parked near the beach and had been allegedly packed with goods. After the relevant parties had arrived at the scene, the container was secured and then removed. The chief asked us to follow up on the number plate, One Kelvin Wright of Abergreen. Martin and I took the short drive over to Mr Wright's property. Mr Wright was a well-known petty criminal to the area who dealt in scrap metal mostly, although you won't find a declared tax bill for that business or any other venture of his. It's a bloody wonder how these bastards get away with it," Fred paused to take a gulp of ale.

"I know, right?" butted in Martin, "My mate Kenny works as a self-employed plumber and the tax people are always on his case! It's one rule for them and..."

"Martin. For god's sake!" Fred interrupted, "Kenny drives a bloody brand-new Range Rover and holidays in the Caribbean three times a year. He's not making that on a plumber's paltry wage. I've told you to stop knocking about with him!"

Martin looked like a child who had turned up to school without his trousers on.

"Anyway," Fred continued, "Kelvin Wright lived on an old farm that had been left to him by his father. The property now resembled something like a long-forgotten scrap yard for a scrap yard. Useless crap everywhere. As we pulled up to his makeshift wire fence, we were not surprised to find the Citroen Berlingo van. After gaining entry to the makeshift graveyard of metal through some improvisation and making sure to keep a wide birth from Kelvin's chained up and very angry Doberman, we knocked on his dilapidated front door. No answer. 'Kelvin! It's the police,' I shouted. Martin here tried the door which was unlocked presumably as not many people came bothering Mr Wright. Well somebody had, as Kelvin Wright's body lay on the kitchen floor with his throat slit and a bloody kitchen knife laying just out of reach. No sign of anyone else in the property, the body was still slightly warm to the touch but in the southern heat of summer, that's not saying much at all. But what I can tell you is the blood had only just started to congeal. Could be suicide I thought, or a botched murder? But why all this over some useless stolen TV's?"

Martin nearly tipped over his chair in a burst of excitement. Hargreaves could see he had been fidgeting with excitement as Fred neared this part of the story. Bless him.

"But the bloody TVs were still in the van!" Martin erupted.

"Yes, thanks Martin." Fred rolled his eyes before continuing,

"So, when we checked sure enough, they were all packed into the little Citroen van. Not many maybe fifteen or so, certainly not worth being murdered over. There was also a large tool chest by the van open and empty. Not an uncommon item for a trade van, however the bolt cutters and broken pad lock by it were suspicious. Why would you need them if the box belonged to you? Together, we opened the box and found blankets, empty water bottles and some rotten food but what really hit us was the stench of human faeces, urine and the rancid odour of unwashed bodies. Obviously, a human being had been living inside this box."

"A stowaway?" Hargreaves asked blandly.

"You'd think so," joined in Martin excitedly.

"Shh! Martin," warned Fred. "I'm telling it. Anyway, we called in the chief and let him know our findings. Now obviously with the amount of flooding and rough seas you wouldn't expect anyone who had been hiding inside a locked box inside another much larger locked box in the Atlantic Ocean to survive now would you? Which is why the chief asked us to contact the fisherman and ask him if he had seen Wright drag the tool chest from the container on the beach the night before. We contacted Mr Steiner using the telephone number provided but were met with an unavailable-number message. The chief told us to keep looking around the property for any other signs of a forced entry or the presumably missing body from the chest, as they were our prime suspect. We found nothing to start with until Martin realised that Mr Wright's dog had been quiet for some time. We went over to the dog's kennel where it was kept on a long length of chain link and followed said chain to behind a nearby shed, it wouldn't have looked out of place in a shanty town. There we found the tool chest's former inhabitant. The dog was unusually distracted and only became aware of us as we walked up close to it. The vicious dog started growling as all dogs do when protecting their food. That's when we saw the badly decomposed half eaten body of a young boy."

"Fuck!!! What the Fuck?" Hargreaves was quite shocked. He had not been expecting the Chuckle Brothers to come out with this story.

Harry leaned over from the bar, while polishing a pint glass. "Please lads! Watch your language," he groaned.

"Sorry Haz," said Fred.

"Yeah, sorry Harry," echoed Martin.

Hargreaves was a bit confused, "Why would he kill himself over it? Surely he'd take his chances with us and admit to a few stolen tellies than kill himself?"

"Naturally we wondered the same thing, Sergeant. But we are very lucky to have DCI Chilcot. He called in forensics, the dead body of the boy was not a refugee or a stowaway at least not from another country and suicide didn't fit in with the injuries Kelvin Wright sustained either. So, there must have been another murderer," Fred explained.

"How so?" Hargreaves asked. How he'd become so captivated by these couple of fucktards he didn't know. Hargreaves himself had been on some pretty dark cases but even he had to admit this one was turning out to be very impressive.

"The child was matched by dental records to a young boy who had been missing from Hackney in London several years ago. Turns out the boy had been visiting his auntie from Hurnsey and had been assumed lost at sea. The boy had reportedly fallen overboard when he had been out on her husband's fishing boat during a particularly bad storm at sea. The body was never found, despite a major search by the police and coastguard. They had no reason to suspect the family especially as the boy's uncle was the first to report it. He himself had been rescued by another fisherman when the boat eventually capsized, throwing him overboard," Fred said with an obvious look of revulsion on his face.

"Guess what the uncle's name was?!" Martin squealed in anticipation.

"Yeah, okay Martin, you can tell the sergeant," Fred said. But Hargreaves had already worked out the answer before Martin said,

"Steiner."

"You see Sergeant, Steiner saw an opportunity to dispose of the boy's body once and for all. At least that's what we suspected as obviously Kelvin Wright wasn't speaking anymore and no one ever saw Steiner or his wife again," Fred swallowed.

"Hang on Fred, I thought DCI Chilcot said..." Martin started to speak before he was interrupted by a kick to his shin from Fred under the table.

"Ow! What was that for?" he moaned whilst rubbing his leg.

Hargreaves was about to ask what that was all about when the two local enforcers stood up from their chairs.

"Hello Chief!" the two uniformed officers chirped.

"Good to see you are all getting on," DCI Chilcot beamed.

Hargreaves hadn't even noticed the DCI come back into the pub. He was far too intrigued to find out what Fred had stopped Martin from spilling.

"Sherlock and Holmes were just about to tell me about this Steiner bloke and what happened to him Chief," Paul tried.

"I heard Sergeant. I think the boys have done a good job of filling you in so far," Chilcot said firmly.

"What was the motive Chief? If the little lad's death was just an accident why didn't his aunt and uncle just tell you the truth at the time?" Paul quizzed.

"Fred here wasn't wrong Sergeant, Mr and Mrs Steiner were never found again. That's not to say that the motive wasn't made crystal clear to us after searching the couple's home, including their computer's hard drive. Need I continue? Surely you can use your own policing skills to deduce what we found and the Steiner's reasons to cover up the death of an innocent young child?" Chilcot said with a look of disgust.

Hargreaves let out a long breath. He would have liked to get his hands on this pair of sick individuals. Still, he thought to himself, there are a few facts with this story that didn't add up. One being the lack of mainstream news coverage of such a case of public interest. He wasn't one to follow much of the goings on in the world – as self-obsessed as he was – however, you couldn't miss some of it being in his job. But before he could form the question in his mind the chief interrupted his thoughts.

"You boys are needed elsewhere I'm afraid. Have you seen Helen yet?"

The two officers groaned like a couple of schoolboys being told to stop playing and come in for tea by their mothers.

"Don't worry lads. You will have plenty more opportunity to spend time with our new sergeant," Chilcot reassured them.

Fred and Martin drained the last of their jars and said their goodbyes.

Martin stood up. "See you later Sergeant Hargreaves." "It's good to finally meet you, Sir," said Fred.

Hargreaves smiled whilst keeping himself seated. This was partly because he didn't want to expose the merry feeling that was now becoming a serious threat to his basic motor skills. Especially in front of the two subservient policemen.

"Call me Paul lads. After all, I'm not on duty until tomorrow," he smugly pointed out whilst giving the DCI a snide glance.

"I still think we should have told him the Packman boy's story," said Martin to Fred.

"Oh, will you stop it, Martin!" replied Fred. "No one wants to hear about two low life drug dealers pimping out those poor girls."

Hargreaves head snapped up in delight ignoring the vertiginous effect it had on him. This was exactly the sort of story he wanted to hear! But before he could dig for more information the chief turned his attention back to the leaving officers.

"That's enough tales from you two for today."

And with that Fred and Martin nodded to Harry and left the tavern through the door, Hargreaves noticed that the spring sun had already began to dip in the sky indicating early evening. It had got late quickly he realised. He really would have to ask them about that story when they were not under the ever-watchful eye of DCI Chilcot.

"Are you hungry Sergeant? Its nearly seven and they do a locally sourced beef welly here."

Hargreaves attention snapped back to the DCI, "No, I'm good ta, I've always been a late eater when I drink. Surely there's a chinky round here or something, or is that asking too much?"

"I believe you mean 'Chinese' and yes, we do Sergeant. Mrs Mei Wing is a wonderful member of our community," Chilcot corrected him as Harry set two more beers down before each of them on the table.

"Two beef wellies please Harry," said Chilcot. "Just try it. If you don't like it, then just leave it. I won't be offended."

"Ok, I'm quite enjoying the beer anyway at the moment."

"Yes, it is good beer, isn't it?" Chilcot smiled. "Now while we wait for our food how about another Colney crime-story?"

"Yeah, go on then," Hargreaves slurred. Another story would be ok. Listening to this fatherly older cop was just like watching a film, wasn't it? He didn't know, he wasn't too sure of much now, but he did want to hear the next damn story!

James Jenkins

MY HUSBANDS MY KEEPER:

Part one

DCI Chilcot held the glass of ale in one hand as the other drummed the tabletop. He looked thoughtfully up at the ceiling.

"Hmm, let me see now…Ah! Ok," the older policeman snapped his fingers and stared back at Hargreaves.

"Now Alice Dawson wasn't born Alice Dawson. Before she married her husband Michael, she was known as Alice Pollard and grew up here in Colney. Alice was a popular girl from a well-liked family in the community. But unfortunately for Alice, around the time of her eighth birthday, her parents and sister were on a family shopping trip to the larger neighbouring town. Tragically they were involved in a mindless crash. A lorry driver who had fallen asleep at the wheel crossed over the lane the family's car was in. The emergency services did their best to try and cut open the wreck of a tin can, but they couldn't save Alice's parents or her sister. Fortunately, although some would argue, Alice had chicken pocks at the time and was staying with her grandmother. A wonderful lady named Rose with a smile as bright as Alice's. Alice stayed with her grandmother who raised her and sent her to university. At nineteen years old, Alice enrolled into a London university and enjoyed the usual and experimental life of a student. It wasn't until her final year that she met a junior doctor, Michael, through a mutual friend. Leaving the party lifestyle behind, she graduated and found solid employment with a local newspaper. They moved in together and supported each other's careers, both worked hours that left little time for each other. This had bothered Alice, sometimes she wondered if they knew each other at all. After a few years of city living, she'd finally had enough and managed to convince a sceptical Michael, to move back to her family home in Colney. She was so excited. Although her poor grandmother had passed away some years before, Alice still had plenty of friends in the town. Remembering one who was perhaps more than a friend gave Alice a prickle of guilt but also a thrill of excitement. For now, she put those thoughts away and remained optimistic about her homecoming. But luck had never been on her side. A month before she and Michael were to move into their new home, a cruel game of fate occurred. On her way back from a visit to Colney, Alice was herself involved in a horrific car accident nearly ending her life. The ambulance rushed her to hospital, she was in a bad way. The medical staff said she would mostly recover but that it would be a long road. Currently she had no feeling in the lower part of her body, but the doctors assured her it was only a temporary condition.

One even suggested it was a psychological matter. Much to her surprise Michael offered to quit his job and take care of her full time. He hadn't been keen on the idea of moving to Colney at all, sighting his work as the biggest factor. For him to give up his only reason to travel back to the city for his daily duties must have been a huge sacrifice for him. Reluctantly, Alice accepted and let Michael arrange for the necessary adaptions to be made to treat Alice properly at home."

"It's very sad and all but where's the pig fucking and dead wives?" The booze was really having its way with Hargreaves now. He was feeling incredibly warm and fuzzy inside. He kept looking at DCI Chilcot and just had an almighty urge to give the large man a big fat hug, an action more justified by that of an early ninety's raver on ecstasy. Fuck! This beer is good he thought. It must be coaxing the crystallised cocaine that still lurked within him.

Chilcot rolled his eyes at the younger man, "Youth of today. No patience, every good story has its build up Sergeant and this one deserves to be told."

"Pleesh go on Guv," Hargreaves' slurring was getting harder for him to control. The stupor was crashing over him in waves, this was currently one of the more drastic moments. Hargreaves made a conscious effort to regain some of his composure allowing the DCI to continue.

"Thank you, Sergeant... Alice moved back into her converted family home, the well-kept beautiful and private manor house down the hill. You know it?"

Hargreaves opted to slowly shake his head rather than trusting his deteriorating verbal skills.

"I'll show you some time. Truly magnificent. Things started well enough, Michael was good and attentive, making sure Alice had all she needed, but it was the times he had to go out that she struggled with the most. As she was still paralyzed from the waist down, Alice couldn't move around. Her body was not yet strong enough to use a wheelchair by herself. The weeks went by and as much as Michael tried to help her, she couldn't get the feeling back into her legs or even begin to try walking again. Alice was sure that the feeling was spreading, getting worse as if moving up through her body from the bottom to the top, like pouring a drink. She told Michael. His patience had been rapidly declining of late she could tell. They had never shared this much time together since uni. 'It's in your head darling. We just need to get working at it.' Michael put down her food. He wasn't the best cook, but he did make a mean casserole. If she could work on her upper body strength, then maybe she could use the wheelchair and do some cooking of her own. Cooking was one of Alice's joys in life, it would certainly go some way towards breaking down the monotony of her days.

Now, it wasn't just the endless boredom that she wanted to keep out of her mind. Alice had a guilty secret she hadn't told Michael, and it was eating her up inside. After seeing a change in him and sacrificing everything he loved with work and the city to look after her, how could she? How could she tell him the reason she had been driving back from Colney that night? She had no reason to have been there without him, some two hundred and fifty miles from their current house at the time. He had never asked either which made the guilt worse. Michael always worked such long shifts and at times they could last a few days when staying away overnight. Because of this it was easy to slip away and make love to her high school sweetheart back in the West Country. All that had stopped now of course. She hadn't even heard from him since she rocked up in an ambulance. Despite feeling like this was her due karma, it was still hard not to feel sorry for herself.

Michael interrupted her thoughts, 'I need to change your dressing and clean your leg, Alice. We don't want it to get infected.' Alice beamed at him, where was this Michael before the accident? She was incredibly squeamish so wouldn't have ever been able to do any of this by herself. Michael had to do all the dressings, injections, bed pan and he would even put a screen over, so she wouldn't have to see the horrific wounds to her legs. They could have afforded to pay for home care, but Michael was adamant that it should be him to look after her. It was no use. She knew she was a terrible person from her affair, it couldn't go on. She had to tell him the truth. She couldn't live with herself otherwise. 'Michael. I need to tell you something.' 'I'm sure it can wait my love. I'll just get your dinner first. I'm sure you need the energy. Pork casserole! For a change.' Alice managed a small laugh secretly relieved by the diversion. 'I'm needed at the office to complete some paperwork for the company,' he explained. 'Can't you just email it to them?' she had asked hopefully. Michael's work had been very understanding when he had tried to hand in his notice. They had made special exceptions for him so that he could carry out most of his duties from home. 'Sorry darling but the papers need to be signed and witnessed in person. Back in the morning, or late afternoon, worst case scenario, ok?' Alice was only mildly shocked. It wasn't that surprising to see some of Michael's old traits creeping back. Still, he deserved a break after what he had done for her, it was just so nice to have him around for a change and he was so compassionate in his bedside manner. She'd barely thought about the friend in the last few days either. 'I've changed your bed pan and left you with plenty of water and snacks. If you need anything just call me.' Before Alice could reply Michael kissed her with perhaps the most passionate kiss that he'd ever given her and with that, he left."

Hargreaves spoke up, "Still sounds like some sickly love story to me Guv. Where's the meat in the sandwich?"

"We were just getting to that Sergeant Hargreaves," Chilcot said with rolling eyes. "So, Alice wakes up after the second morning in a row and still her husband hadn't come home. Ideally, she would have liked to try calling his mobile phone countless times over the past evening and now this morning just for some reassurance of when he would be arriving back home. But alas she couldn't seem to find hers anywhere to hand. Alice was beginning to get hungry and thirsty by this point. Those water bottles and cereal bars will only get you so far. Plus, Alice was pretty concerned about her own leg as there seemed to be quite a foul smell coming from it. However, she could nearly use her upper body strength now and was sure she could feel pins and needles in her legs again. This gave her a glimmer of hope that all was not as bad as previously feared. She would have preferred to be able to share this positive news with Michael though. Psyching herself up, Alice braced herself for the unpretty sight. The wound needed dressing every day and it had now been two days since it was looked after by Michael. Using all her strength Alice bent down towards her legs. This was the first time she had been able to sit up since the hospital and instantly she knew something wasn't right as her head swam from the exertion.

Nothing could prepare Alice for the impending horror as she pulled back the sheets."

Harry came over to the table where the two officers sat.

"Here's your food lads. Hope you enjoy it."

"Thank you, Harry," Chilcot replied. "I'm just filling our new sergeant in on some of the more serious cases around Colney and our neighbouring communities."

The plates of food wobbled in the landlord's calloused hands. Hargreaves watched with distaste as the man's thumb sunk into the gravy on one of the plates.

"Oh, do tell him about what old Davey Turner found up at the old schoolhouse. The one that posh family from the city moved into for a while, that's a good story," Harry chirped in with excitement.

"I'm trying to fixate on more hard crime cases that contain evidence rather than hearsay Harry."

"Wow, hang on a minute, what's all this about?" enquired Hargreaves.

"As you're taking a surprise interest in Colney's history Sergeant I'll let Harry tell you. But remember what I said. It is only hearsay, so don't go twisting the truth any more than Davey Turner no doubt already has, Harry."

"Oh, come on now DCI Chilcot. You know Davey Turner's not one to tell mistruths," said Harry.

"Yeah, come on Guv. This sounds good, you can come back to Mrs dreary doors and her nurse husband in a minute…" Paul was feeling very jolly now. The beer certainly had an intoxicating effect not too dissimilar from the narcotics he was so used to consuming. Was that his tongue beginning to feel the slight numbness of baby teething powder? Either way it prompted Hargreaves to do something quite out of character.

"Sorry about our misunderstanding earlier mate."

Hargreaves put his hand out to Harry temporarily forgetting the gravy covered thumb. He was too preoccupied in directing the limb to its desired point of contact. Harry placed the food in front of the two- policemen giving Hargreaves the thumbed plate.

"Oh, you see, I don't believe it was a misunderstanding Sergeant. I believe it was just plain rudeness on your part.

However, as the chief here will tell you I'm not one to harbour grudges. Your choice of vocabulary could still do with some polishing though." Harry took Paul's hand which remained limp in the landlord's grip.

"Err, yeah whatever mate," Hargreaves replied. Before he had time to work out if the old landlord was testing him or not Harry started to talk.

"It's only a short tail and will perhaps give DCI Chilcot here a few minutes to eat his meal before he continues." Harry pulled up a chair at the table to begin his story.

James Jenkins

A BRIEF INTERRUPTION

"See it's not uncommon for new folk to move to Colney, however, they never tend to stay long for one reason or another. Me I can't understand it personally, but then not everyone had the reason the Mason's did. Not long after they had moved into the old schoolhouse that had been converted into a large and luxurious family house, they left to go on holiday. As Davey Turner was their ground keeper of sorts, they had asked him to keep a keen eye on the place in their absence. One-day Davey turns up to prune the bushes and as he passes the outdoor pool, on a blisteringly warm summer's day, he spots the Mason's son and an attractive young lady fornicating in the pool. Now Davey had met the lad on a handful of occasions before, so he didn't panic. The Mason's had told Davey that their son might even be about whilst they were away as he was on summer holidays from university. Before Davey could turn on his heel and get out of the garden young Master Mason's female companion spotted Davey and looked incredibly distressed. She quickly exited the pool and grabbed a towel to cover her modesty or what was left of it. That was the last Davey saw of the Mason's boy and he was too embarrassed himself to go back to the house.
After five or six weeks, when the couple finally arrived back from their holidays Mrs Mason called Davey and asked him if he could come and look at some gooseberry bushes that were being attacked by birds. Davey went around to the Mason's house and after accepting a cuppa from Mrs Mason whilst discussing the best way to protect her fruits from the harm of birds, a young lady in her teens walked into the room. Davey

couldn't believe it! It must be young Master Mason's girlfriend he thought feeling the blood rush to his cheeks. Clearly the girl recognised Davey as she turned an even prettier shade of red before rushing out of the room. 'Sarah?' Mrs Mason called after her. 'Sorry Mr Turner I don't know what's come over my daughter of late. She only just came back from travelling the other week and hasn't been the same since. Would you mind coming back later?' Davey practically had to drag his jaw out of the Mason's house."

Hargreaves couldn't hide his glee, "She was fucking her brother?! What the fuck is wrong with you people?"

"Ok that's enough Harry, I don't think the sergeant here needs anymore reason to think everyone in Colney are a bunch of inbreeds than he already does," DCI Chilcot interjected.

"You got that right Guv! You lot are one banjo short of a hillbilly's gangbang!" Hargreaves laughed unable to stop himself.

"Hang on a minute. They weren't from round here. They weren't local," protested Harry.

DCI Chilcot watched Hargreaves' besmirching grin and rolled his eyes at the bibulous sergeant.

"Using those sorts of lines aren't doing us the best service to change that stereotype either Harry."

"Sorry Chief. Well, I'll let you boys get back to your serious crime talk. What one is it you're telling him about Chief?" Harry enquired.

"Alice."

Harry was taken aback looking at the DCI with genuine concern.

"Are you sure Chief? I mean that's… you know?" Harry's eyes darted briefly at the clearly inebriated Paul Hargreaves.

"It is very important to me that Sergeant Hargreaves understands the community before he can become *a part of it* Harry."

"Ok Chief, it's your choice," Harry said before shuffling back to his bar. Hargreaves watched the landlord who kept looking back over his shoulder towards the DCI, a concerned look on his face.

Hargreaves had found himself emotionally aroused by the landlord's story, not physically though. Strange he thought, normally that sort of story would give Hargreaves at least a semi. But he couldn't feel much between his legs at all now or anywhere in that region he realised. Must be the beer. It was fucking good beer! Shame that Harry had to sour the mood though.

"So, where's the little slut now Boss? Sounds like she would be gagging for it!" Hargreaves slurred.

"Enough Sergeant! I won't tolerate that sort of attitude from one of my officers. And wipe that drool from off your mouth!"

Hargreaves lifted his arm to his mouth failing to connect until the third swipe of his chin. The beer was certainly leaving its mark on him.

"Sorry Boss, I'm only kidding. Just can't see there being much action for a single bloke round here," Hargreaves said. As the DCI took a long swig of his pint the sergeant surveyed the room. Most of the punters had left the pub. Not too surprising he thought, the sun had long settled down for the night and it must have been getting late. The funny thing was he hadn't noticed anyone leave since the two policemen earlier.

"For the record, both of the Mason's children never returned to the town again and the parents sold the house shortly after. So at least that's one young woman you won't be defiling Sergeant. Now shall we get back to poor Alice and what she found under her bed sheets?"

"Yes Sir," replied Hargreaves slightly puzzled about where that last remark came from.

James Jenkins

MY HUSBANDS MY KEEPER:

Part two

"Ok. But before we can return to Alice, I need to tell you about one of our neighbouring police departments. The officers were informed by a concerned homeowner that a suspicious figure had been walking along a path that led to the resident's private beach. The witness was adamant that the trespasser had been struggling to carry a heavy object over one shoulder. When our boys in blue arrived to survey the scene, they found two bodies on the beach. Both appeared to have fallen from the steep incline. I have seen the area myself and can confirm that the path is treacherous in daylight, let alone the middle of the night. One of the bodies had serious head trauma, the injuries associated with a fall from the rockface. Paramedics were unable to resuscitate the man who died at the scene. Later it would be confirmed that this was Michael Dawson. The other body which was wrapped in tarpaulin had been dead for some time, rigor mortis already under way."

"Now we're talking."

"Quite, Sergeant. A car was found close by at the scene, seemingly abandoned. When officers ran the plates, they found that it was registered to one Andrew Parkhurst of Colney town."

Hargreaves gasped almost choking on the excess saliva in his mouth, "I bet he was the bloke Alice was shagging! Her old man knocked him off?"

"Sergeant Hargreaves your crime deducing abilities are second to none. It's a wonder you haven't made DCI yourself by now!" Chilcot said sarcastically. "I'm afraid as I have told you before. Not everything is as simple as it seems. You must have learnt this before now with such a glowing record as you claim to have?"

"It would have been enough for me Boss," Hargreaves offered.

He was really having to concentrate on his every syllable now, continuing to fight his slurring speech.

"Perhaps that's your problem Paul. Not everything is as black and white as the police cars of old. Hopefully it's not too late to teach you a thing or two Sergeant Hargreaves. Anyway, Andrew Parkhurst had a wife who came and identified his body."

Hargreaves noticed the way the chief seemed to struggle when he said Andrew Parkhurst's name. It was the second time he had done it. It was just a hint of something but nothing more.

The DCI's characteristically steely demeanour returning, "Naturally Mrs Parkhurst was distraught at the death of her husband as was her young daughter. Mr Parkhurst didn't have any enemies according to his wife and she didn't recognise the name Michael Dawson or his photo. Mr Parkhurst worked as an orderly in a private nursing home about thirty miles away from Colney and was due to do a two-day night shift, so it wasn't unlike him to be away for a length of time. The residents needed round the clock care and his wife had come to expect her husband's shifts to run over. She didn't even know he was missing at the time. Police checked with his work who said although it was unusual for Andrew, they were used to having a high staff turnover. Especially due to the nature of the job and low pay. So, they just called someone else on shift. The police had nothing to go on, there was nothing connecting the two men together."

"Well it's got to be Alishes... Sorry Al-is-sis boyfriend schurely?" Hargreaves silently cursed his struggling tongue and attempted to carry on speaking.

"No woman ever believes her husband is cheating. Blokes are just too good at it. Fuck knews I've never bin cot."

"If you carry on with that stance in life Sergeant you are sure to be found out sooner or later," Chilcot warned the tongue-tied sergeant.

"Hmph," Hargreaves grumbled, not believing the more experienced officer for a second that the great Paul Hargreaves ever would. Not that he had ever been soppy enough to have had what he'd describe as a girlfriend. There had been plenty of fucking though. Oh yes, he purred privately. He was a pro! "I worked undercover for two years and no one suspected a thing!" Maybe this old boy didn't know anything about Paul's demotion and the photos the press had been holding on to.

"Meanwhile, back to Alice, who was trying to come to terms with what she had discovered under the goose and down bed covers, of which had played an unwilling part by hiding the stark truth."

Hargreaves erupted, "What?! C'mon Chief! Stop beating around the bush. What did she find?"

DCI Chilcot looked deep into Hargreaves' bloodshot eyes pausing before abruptly and yet calmly saying, "Her left leg had been removed from just below the thigh."

"Fuck off!" If Hargreaves could have moved them his hands would have covered his mouth in shock surprise.

"The stump had been well bandaged," DCI Chilcot continued. "But after a couple days of neglect it had become saturated and oozed out from the tightly wrapped gauze. I can't imagine what Alice must have felt at that precise moment, but I can tell you what she told me. Her first thought was that Michael had not told her to keep it from her, to protect her. It didn't make sense though. Although she had been in and out of consciousness after leaving the hospital, she could swear she remembered it being there. Plus, the way the wound was oozing suggested this was more recent than the accident. Maybe it had become gangrenous and Michael had to amputate, he had been a surgeon before taking a less messy role as a consultant for a private health care company. He would have never done anything as risky as that at home though, and why? Unless Michael had found out about her affair. But surely, he wouldn't do something like that to her and if he wanted revenge why would he keep it from her? Alice was now realising that she really didn't know her husband at all. Naturally it took some time to compose herself and get out of that bed. With her husband forgetting to put her phone in reach or not putting her phone in reach on purpose, she knew she had to try and move. After what could have been hours and an empty stomach from all the vomiting from shock and disgust, Alice rolled herself out of the bed. The feeling in her lower body and remaining leg was coming back more now and found she could even move the remaining leg slightly. But with this returning sensation also came the agony of the amputated leg, or the stump more specifically.

Why was she suddenly getting her feeling back? What had Michael used on her? Was she ever paralyzed in the first place? Who knew what a respected doctor could do to alter medical records? The fear and paranoia increased. Perhaps it was this desire to find out that gave her the strength to drag herself to the kitchen. Alice struggled with all her might gritting her teeth and bending back the fingernails on her hands, scratching at the floorboards to get purchase. Pushing on through the pain and effort, she grabbed the telephone cord. From her horizontal position the heavy landline phone crashed down from the table and onto the floor beside her. Fortunately, it didn't smash to pieces. Alice immediately called an ambulance who also sent a police officer over to her. Whilst she waited for their arrival, she pulled open the fridge door and managed to find some left-over pork inside. Maybe it had turned slightly in the few days she had waited but Alice didn't care. She was famished, she stuffed handfuls of it into her mouth before passing out.

The next time Alice woke up she was in a hospital bed with two police officers sitting by her."

LOCAL CUISINE

DCI Chilcot finished the last of his beer savouring the liquid in his mouth before swallowing. Hargreaves hadn't even noticed his own so engrossed as he was. DCI Chilcot set his empty glass back down before continuing his account.

"Some hours passed but eventually Alice showed signs of consciousness. After the doctors and staff had descended upon Alice like ants on a sugar cube, they declared her fit enough to talk with the two officers. They asked Alice to identify a picture of her husband and explained what they all knew about the all-but-confirmed murderer, Michael Dawson and his activity over the last few days, up until his end. Michael had left a lot of unanswered questions. They told Alice about Andrew Parkhurst, her lover's unfortunate brother: she had been too numb to cry. The doctors told Alice that the surgery performed on her leg was that of a professional and if wasn't for the few days of neglect, it would have healed fine. They had very little to do other than clean the wound. Although the medical professionals in counselling and physical rehabilitation would still have their work cut out for them.
Understandably Alice was broken in more ways than one. What she couldn't work out was why he had carried this on for months, why not just kill her instead of cutting off her leg? Of course, she knew Andrew Parkhurst but how could Michael know who he was? To make things worse the evil bastard had died so she would never be able to ask him."

"What about this Parkhurst then? I thought you said there was more to it. Why did Michael kill him if he wasn't shagging Alice?" Hargreaves asked noticing the handle on his speech was for now under control.

DCI Chilcot looked visibly offended at Hargreaves' last statement. He composed himself and carried on, "I will get to that Paul, please just listen."

Hargreaves looked at the old man. He looked like he was trembling, he hadn't looked like that before. Maybe the beer was getting to the old chief too he wondered. Should be, he thought. He could barely move his own arms now and couldn't remember the last time he moved his legs. "Oh well Pauly boy! Enjoy the high," he advised himself. The words seemed to swim around his head.

"The police had worked out that Andrew Parkhurst was murdered on the night before Mr Dawson supposedly left for work. Judging by the slight decomposition of the body Andrew Parkhurst was most likely murdered by strangulation, two days prior to this. The night the police found Michael Dawson was the night after he told Alice he left to visit the office. The next question changed Alice's life forever. Alice would never be the same again.

The police officer in charge of the questioning was perhaps not the most experienced to deal with the situation. But then who would be? All he could do was look to his colleague for support. Obvious nerves led him to naturally address her with her married name. 'Mrs Dawson…' 'Mrs Pollard!' Alice had spat. 'Don't ever call me by that bastard's name again!' The officer didn't look at his partner this time, he just drew a breath, 'Sorry Mrs Pollard. Alice. Can I call you Alice?"

Parochial Pigs

"Fucken ell Guf. Never mind what they called her jus spit it out!" Hargreaves was really on the edge of his seat now. At least he would be if he could make his limbs work. Fuck! I'm wankered, he realised, not even noticing his latest vocal mishap. Chilcot looked over his pint at Hargreaves. "Did that cheeky wanker just laugh at me?" Paul wondered.

"Patience Hargreaves," Chilcot said, "Let me continue. The police officer carried on with the mandatory questions. 'Alice,' he began, 'Have you any idea why your husba... ahem, Mr Dawson would have any reason to murder Mr Parkhurst? So far all we have as a motive is Mr Parkhurst's car. Michael Dawson's fingerprints were found on the steering wheel'. The officer showed her a picture of the Vauxhall Corsa that had belonged to Andrew. Alice didn't think her life could have hit a further low until this point. You see Sergeant, Alice recognised the car straight away. It was the very same Corsa her lover had been driving the last time they had met."

"Told you! I knew they were fucking!"

"NO!" the DCI bellowed. He calmed himself, taking a couple breaths.

Hargreaves looked at the superior crime guru. "He's fucking losing it," Paul chuckled to his inner self.

DCI Chilcot now composed, spoke again, "Alice had been sleeping with his brother..."

"Shit! Well where's he been all this time? Some cunt he is letting his brother get whacked for him!"

Chilcot suddenly stood up from his chair. "SHUT THE FUCK UP SERGEANT. WILL YOU SHUT THE FUCK UP?!"

Now tensing his arms by his side, on the edge of hyperventilating, tears began to form in the corners of the DCI's eyes.

Hargreaves bristled. He looked around the room as best as his tired neck would let him, the bar was empty except the two of them and the chink of glasses in some other room, presumably Harry. When had that happened?

"Chief I'm so sorry, I didn't mean anything by it. I get it. You know these people. I didn't mean for you to get all het up about it."

Chilcot picked up his chair which had fallen on its back after his sudden upheaval and sat down closing his eyes as he did. When he opened them, he was the same calm and confident man Hargreaves had first met.

"It's nothing. I suppose you're right, to be fair Paul," Chilcot said.

"Anyway, Alice's actual lover had been working away. When all this tragedy had unravelled, he was uncontactable. The night of Alice's car crash, she had met him at a seemingly innocuous bar. They had talked about her ending things with Michael but as he was always away it had become hard to approach the topic. The move to Colney came around quicker than she could believe. On the night Alice was to meet her high school sweetheart to discuss her plans to break off the affair, the conversation had not gone well. He had wanted to make a go of things. He knew Michael was never right for her. But he had let it go for her sake. Travelling back in his brother Andrew's car he'd borrowed for the night, as he was staying in Colney for the holidays. Alice's lover decided he would give her what she wanted and the very next day he accepted a case that would take him away for what could be a very long time. He would later come to regret that decision… but then somethings are meant to be. Later that night Alice was run off the road by a hit and run driver. It's unlikely this was a coincidental attack now knowing what we do about Michael Dawson".

"You sound like you know these people well Boss," Hargreaves managed.

"Alice was my first love Hargreaves, my wife now. I am Andrew's stepbrother; he and I shared the same mother… but he paid the price for lending me his car and so did his wife and daughter as I stripped them of a good husband and father. Michael Dawson had followed me when I met up with Alice that night and that's what I now have to live with."

Hargreaves couldn't move. Literally he had now lost almost all his basic motor functions by this point. He just remained slack jawed in awe of this revelation.

"…and do you know the worst thing, Sergeant?"

Hargreaves wobbled his head from side to side, he was dribbling a little bit again as well. "No," he struggled the one syllable out of his mouth.

"There was never any pork in that fridge or that casserole."

Hargreaves stomach did cartwheels. He should have eaten his food. Instead, his beef wellington was just looking cold and congealed in front of him. But then stories of force-fed cannibalism will do that to you.

# THE GIRL AND THE MISSING SCARECROW

"You're going to have to excuse me for the minute Sergeant..." Chilcot said as he stood up from his chair, "...little call of nature needs answering."

Hargreaves forced a nod. The superior officer entered the gents leaving Hargreaves to his thoughts. After what seemed like an unreasonably long amount of time for someone to take a simple toilet break, Chilcot walked back to the table. Hargreaves had been trying to concentrate on retracting the now very long and thick cascade of drawl that was hanging from his chin, unfortunately for Hargreaves, he had been completely unsuccessful. When was the last time he'd pissed? Normally Hargreaves had the bladder of a racehorse, but right now couldn't tell if he needed it at all.

"Looks like someone couldn't wait hey Sergeant?" Chilcot chuckled as he walked back over to the table. Hargreaves followed the chief's eyes which had settled on a damp patch on the carpeted floor running up the inside of his expensive trouser leg. "What?" Hargreaves mumbled.

"It's ok Sergeant, happens to the best of us. Especially when you are not used to the strong Devonshire ale," Chilcot said with some sympathy.

Parochial Pigs

"Your modesty is at least safe for the time being as Harry is about to shut the pub for the night. A lock in on your first day Sergeant! What a privilege."

Hargreaves tried to get up, but his body wouldn't listen to the message his brain was trying to send. He tried to wipe the dangling saliva from his mouth that was now only millimetres from the tabletop, but his arms just flopped about at his sides. What was wrong with him? If he didn't know better, he would think he was being stitched up. Surely the beer couldn't be this strong. DCI Chilcot sat back down at the table sensing Paul's distress.

"Don't panic Sergeant. I haven't met anyone yet who could handle Harry's "Special ale". Especially not the first time of trying. I'm sure you will be good as new by the morning."

"Arrghuf..." Paul strained.

"What's that Sergeant? Oh yes!" the DCI smiled coolly.

"Don't go worrying about that missing scarecrow now. I'm sure between the both of us we can get to the bottom of it. I knew you would always be a big asset to the town Paul, I just need to educate you better, so you know how to contribute more effectively to the community."

Hargreaves had no idea what the old chief was on about. He couldn't even talk anymore; he didn't feel all that drunk but then he didn't really care either. Maybe the DCI was right – he would wake up ok in the morning. Just some backward police department's idea of an initiation process. That old wanker at the bar was probably in on it too, the whole town was probably laughing behind his back. "Oh, I'll get my own back you little piggy fuckers," he promised himself. Nothing he could do now about it but let the chief have his moment.

"Before we can solve the missing scarecrow case Paul, I need to tell you one more story. Now this case is a very sad one and like Harry's story about the Mason family, you won't find this one in the police archives. Not entirely anyway. Our story takes place out of Colney in a city. Which city isn't important right now, but a city it was."

BROKEN GOODS

"Little Hannah hadn't had it easy growing up. After Hannah's father had passed away before his time her mum moved them both to the city in which she had lived before Colney. Now Hannah's mother had been a wild child before she married, I suppose it was inevitable that she would wind up mixing with the bad sorts she used to know. An ex-flame who was now regarded as a moderately successful drug dealer. Due to the disturbing circumstances regarding Hannah's lack of father in her life, her mother hadn't taken it well. What started out as a crutch for her mother's pain soon became an addiction. Heavy drinking and recreational cannabis use were soon replaced with harder drugs and harder characters. Now Hannah's mum was a very attractive woman for her age, so she was in favour to this dealer who saw more than a mutual attraction in her. You see Sergeant, as we both know, victims like Hannah's mum are easy pickings for the scum of the underworld.

The mother was happy for now, albeit at the expense of her child's wellbeing. Poor Hannah was dragged along with her mother to the crack-house-squalors. Her mother's money had quickly dissipated and the three-bed house in Colney was a distant memory. But Hannah counted herself lucky when her mum left her alone in their deprived flat. At least it meant she didn't have to see the stupor her mother would end up in, letting herself become prey to undesirable men. The mother had become cold and indifferent to Hannah over the past years since her husband's death. The drug and alcohol abuse effecting her moods and tempers daily. Sometimes her mother would shout at the young girl to stay in her bedroom telling the poor little child who hadn't even seen her tenth birthday yet, that she reminded her too much of her father. This wasn't helped by the resemblance she bore to him. It wasn't long before Hannah and her mother were evicted from their flat forcing them to take refuge in the scum bag dealer's dwellings. Many drug addicts and other less desirables visited that house. So, with Hannah's mother and her new boyfriend usually intoxicated beyond sanity or capability to parent, it is easy, yet very sickening to imagine the life and abuse that a young girl would experience.

Now I can't be sure if little Hannah suffered at the hands of the washed-up dregs of society, only Hannah herself could have told us that and from what I know she has never shared very much of the experiences endured in that disgusting house of sin. What I do know, is the drug pusher's charity for the mother only ran so far. You see this foul man saw a new enterprise for Hannah's mother. God knows what that woman was forced to endure with Hannah only a few feet away. Some might even say she deserved it for what she put her daughter through just for a quick high. But then, who am I to judge?"

Hargreaves croaked a little but nothing that would have counted for English. His head had slumped slightly to the side and the steady stream of drool hanging from his mouth had reached the table top some time ago as it now formed a pool on the wooden surface. Hargreaves had given up trying to move his... well his anything really. He was totally numb. He would say comfortably numb as he really did feel good, but he was wondering if he should have had that last beer. It didn't much matter now, he couldn't pick his pint up if he wanted to.

"What was that, Sergeant? The beer has really gone to your head, tonight hey?"

Chilcot looked smug, Hargreaves realised. The older man carried on as if nothing had happened, "Heroes can come in the most unlikely of characters, but this particular one was a hero no less. An anonymous call was made to the police about a young girl who was suffering from malnutrition and being neglected. The address they gave matched that of the house Hannah now lived in with her mother. It was later found out that the informant, was a man who was known to the police as a suspect curb crawler and had previously been convicted for solicitation of a prostitute. As a way of trying to lighten his sentence he confessed it was himself who had called in with the information regarding Hannah's wellbeing. It was *after* his visit he'd apparently realised the poor girl had been hiding under the bed for the duration. He claimed to have never returned to the house again to do anymore *business*. Apparently, even perverts have a conscience. Paraphernalia and small quantities of drugs were found in the house but nothing strong enough to raise a conviction against the drug peddler. Apart from the poor hygiene and malnutrition, Hannah appeared to be physically unharmed. A very dedicated social worker wasn't going to let her stay another night in that drug den though. She managed to get authority to take the girl away that night and left a rather intoxicated and abusive mother behind, standing at the front door yelling obscenities whilst being held back by two police officers. This social worker was another hero although she has never been able to see it any other way than her moral duty. Hannah's mother was found hanging from the banister of the run-down house two days later. Inquiries were made but the wannabe pimp's original statement held and after all he was the one who called the police! He even had three witnesses who had been round his house and found the body hanging there. A pity, the police would have been happy to get this stain on society off the streets, but nothing would stick."

"Eeeiiiiiiii," Hargreaves' mouth emitted. He liked this story! Sergeant Paul Hargreaves could have made it stick on this bastard, he was sure. "I might pass out in a minute," he thought to himself. His sight had become tunnel like. His peripheral vision all but disappearing. It was like seeing everything before you on a T.V. screen that was slowly moving further and further away while blackness crept in around the edges.

"I thought this one would be your type of thing Sergeant!" Chilcot snidely said. "Stick with me Paul. There's plenty more drama to come."

"After poor little Hannah found out about her mother, as you can imagine, the child was distraught. The disturbed woman was all the little girl had ever known of her family since the death of her father. Hannah had been only very young at the time so held no solid memories of her life before. Oh, the social workers were brilliant. The original lady who got her away from that hell hole was incredibly attentive. But these people have their own lives too Paul. Their own children and husbands and when that clocking off time comes it was another new face for Hannah on shift. Times have changed Hargreaves, social care and children's wellbeing has come a long way but unfortunately for Hannah, this had not come quick enough. The poor girl had no other living relatives or dependants that the authorities could contact. They did find out about an uncle, but he'd been away working and wasn't contactable at this stage. I hear they tried, but as we both know, certain employment dictates it. If he had known, then I can most certainly vouch for him, mountains would have been moved to intervene.

Naturally Hannah found herself moving from one foster home to another finding some glimpses of happiness but never anywhere she could feel home. I'm led to believe she was well looked after in these foster homes. After the death of her mother coupled with her father – Andrew Parkhurst – early departure from this world, what she needed was a family."

Hargreaves' eyes flickered at the name. He was willing his mind to put it all together, but the chief just carried on, "That unconditional love that can be found in most homes wasn't offered to her until it was too late. As you know, or at least should do Sergeant, in our line of work the life of an undercover officer is that of incredible sacrifice.

Those with families rarely go into these positions due to the isolation from their usual life. You already know from the story about my wife, that I had taken a position that would see me go away for some time, well I had committed to an undercover operation that would eventually take eight precious years of my life away from me. After discovering about the death of my brother and his wife, I received the news concerning Alice. I rushed to see Alice; I couldn't believe it Paul. All of it, my fault!"

Chilcot slammed his meaty fist on to the table, knocking his and the sergeant's pints over. The liquid spilled onto Hargreaves' unresponsive and already moistened lap.

"Bit rude," Hargreaves thought.

"My Brother! His poor wife and precious daughter! And the woman who I had always loved. Alice and I talked extensively; I won't go into details Paul; this is not Alice's, nor my, story. It is Hannah's. Without hesitation we both agreed to adopt my niece and make our own life together. Hannah's miserable upbringing was my burden, not that either my wife or I ever saw it as such. Still, it wasn't any easy process and it took more than just time alone. Eventually Hannah moved in with us, back in her hometown of Colney and as hard as it might be, I reminded myself that I owed this to Andrew at the very least. Perhaps even her mother despite her poor choices. You see Paul, I always think that we are responsible for the choices we make despite the hardships life throws at us."

Hargreaves couldn't get his head around it all. This was a heavy story to be telling someone on a first date. "First date? Fuck. Where am I?" he worried to himself. "Oh yeah! That old DCI'S telling me about his niece." Still a tad strange though. There was more to this than his usual deduction skills could fathom in his current state.

"You could tell from early on that Hannah was going to be a hard girl to raise. Her upbringing had obviously affected her far worse that she let on. Rarely ever did she open to anyone, although we did what we thought was our best by her. It wasn't really a surprise that as she barely reached her eighteenth birthday, Hannah ran away. I can't hide from the facts: a career policeman of my background should have seen it coming.

With a few belongings packed inside her backpack, Hannah boarded a train for the city. I suppose this was what she wanted, a fresh start. To break away from the sleepy life of Colney and the constant reminder of her past. At eighteen years of age, she had outgrown her town and yearned for more. Her upbringing was far from straight forward but eventually she had learnt she had all the love and support from her legal guardians that any girl could wish for. But it still hadn't stopped Hannah from wanting something more. Now, she was a bright girl, but as result of the turbulence she had experienced as a child, school life was not easy for her. When compulsory education had ended, she lacked any proper qualifications. Perhaps naivety played a part, but Hannah relied heavily on her beauty and had been offered an audition for a modelling agency. After arriving in the city and using her small savings to secure a bed and breakfast for the next two months, Hannah went to the agency for her interview. The whole thing was a complete scam. They get these poor girls to pay around two-hundred pounds a time for a portfolio. Anyway, Hannah didn't have the money but as she was leaving, heard some of the other disgruntled applicants talking about a freelance photographer who might be able to help with a portfolio. He had also claimed to have contacts with magazine publishers looking for models. Now, I'm pretty sure you're thinking the same thing as me sergeant. Top shelf. Blue movies. That type of thing but this didn't work out too badly for Hannah. The shoots were mainly small-time adverts, the occasional dear Deirdre column. You know the one that's like a photo comic strip? My wife loved them."

"gug gug…" Hargreaves trembled out with more saliva to follow. He had known a girl once who had done something similar.

"So, the extra work and the decent enough pay afforded Hannah a small flat. All was going well. She had even tried to reassure Alice and me sending a brief letter about the horrific way she had left. 'I'll come back home soon and make my peace with you. I just need to find my own way.' It didn't work out that way unfortunately and things took a turn for the worse when Hannah stopped receiving phone calls. Now it could be argued that around this time she had been following the trend of the other girls in the business and had started to use drugs, but as we know about Hannah's past some will say it was inevitable. This wasn't her first brush with narcotics either as my wife and I were used to finding paraphernalia in her room. The drug abuse had not been kind on Hannah as it rarely is on anyone. The late nights leading to turning up late. I'm told the calls just stopped coming. Before she knew it, the rent was up. There was no money left to pay for it. She didn't feel she could go home. Not like this, it would hurt her pride far too much. Unfortunately, her pride led her into the hands of one Bobby Cavendish."

Hargreaves moved his... well no, he didn't move anything. He couldn't, by this point he was totally numb all over. No! He wasn't numb. Hargreaves was paralyzed! That made him think he should remember something, why did that seem familiar to him now. He wasn't thinking properly, everything was slowing down. Bobby Cavendish! How did this Chilcot know about him? Cavendish was one of the biggest players in Bristol's underworld. A nightclub and property owner, he proclaimed, but a glorified pimp and drug dealer was more accurate. Cavendish had built himself a solid illegal crime base over the years, his reach was a powerful one. He was also a very wanted man by Bristol police force. Hargreaves didn't want to think about Bobby Cavendish anymore. He wanted to go home. Screw the police force, this Chilcot either knew more about Hargreaves' career problems or this was a very big coincidence. The fact that his new boss was allowing him to stew in his own stinking piss and spilt beer led him to believe it was probably not the latter.

"Now you may be wondering Hargreaves, how could I know all of this? My own hands were tied, my face was a well-known one on the streets of Bristol. No doubt you're familiar with my previous role in the vice squad there? To find Hannah would mean moving with severe caution so not to scare her away again. I had to use someone I could trust who knew Hannah as well as I did but who wouldn't be recognised by anyone from the criminal underworld. With my contacts exhausted I became overly reliant on my wife. I was blinded by my own guilt of losing my brother's daughter and my usually rational mind hadn't considered the danger I had put them in. I think, between us, we would have perhaps given up, or more likely tried a different angle.

That was until we found a tiny glimmer of hope. A small but obvious detail. Hannah had changed her name. No wonder we hadn't had any luck finding her.

Cavendish had a liking for Hannah. He'd seen her pictures. He was overjoyed to learn she had run into some financial difficulty and was struggling to make good on some money owed. I don't always claim to know what goes on in these fucking twisted low life's minds Paul, even with the extensive training we are privy to within criminal psychology these days. Maybe it was a case of love at first sight or maybe it was just pure and simple lust on his part.

Whatever it was, Cavendish had acted quickly. He sent one of his employees to see her and offered her a job in his club. All very classy and very well paid, she wouldn't have to do anything that she didn't feel comfortable with. This was special treatment indeed as the other girls who worked there were nowhere near as fortunate. Cavendish didn't own a night club Paul. He owned a seedy lap dance club which was known for its extra services."

Hargreaves didn't even bother trying this time. He just remained still. He knew Cavendish's lap dancing bar inside and out. He also knew about their "extra services" of which he was very well accustomed.

"Hannah was desperate, and she certainly wasn't shy. She accepted the job on the spot on the promise that it was meeting and greeting work only, nothing else. On her first day of work she met one of Cavendish's associates at the club, a man already familiar to her by this point. All went well, she made a killing in tips and the regulars loved her. It made her feel good about herself I think, even though she knew some of the other girls did more than dancing. Having everyone fixating on her, especially one of Bobby's employees who gave her all the attention she had craved as a child. Cavendish seemed happy with things, he had met her and left Hannah to it from what I hear. He regularly received updates on her from his staff and made sure she was being treated with respect. Maybe he wasn't so bad after all? All was good until Cavendish's associate and Hannah started a... romance would be doing it far too much justice."

"Oh shit!" thought Hargreaves.

"Poor Hannah..." DCI Chilcot shook his head with great sadness.

"Or Emily as I believe you knew her. She would never find out that her new boyfriend was a police officer working undercover to investigate Bobby Cavendish."

Sergeant Paul Hargreaves realised he was going to die tonight.

"One Dicky Farrell no less. Of course, we both know him as Sergeant Paul Hargreaves."

It was abundantly obvious to Hargreaves that it was not going to be a pleasant death.

James Jenkins

I'D DO IT ALL AGAIN

At least he couldn't feel anything. He remembered the girl very well indeed. Emily wasn't the type of girl you forgot. She had been right up Hargreaves' street. It was made all the better by the fact that Cavendish had put her off limits. Hargreaves didn't care though. It was all part of the challenge. He had his pickings from the other girls at the club. It was his favourite bit of this undercover lark, after the free drugs obviously! Hargreaves' superiors had been asking for some evidence with increasing pressure lately and he was still failing to deliver. He hadn't wanted the fun to stop and perhaps he realised, it was far too late to end his involvement now. Several attempts to pass off other small-time players in Cavendish's empire had failed to satisfy his superiors. Still, at least he had managed to get into Cavendish's little tart's knickers. Someone had to break her in. He had bragged to the other girls about it, something that had backfired on him as he now realised their loyalty was to Cavendish and not him. Surely it was them at fault for his current predicament. Jealous bitches he thought. Hargreaves had even broken his cover to a handful of the girls, such was his arrogance. He had believed that using intimidation of long prison sentences or threatening to name them as informers would have certainly led to the individual's untimely deaths.

"Poor Emily must have believed that she had finally found love. That was until she saw what Dicky had been up to with one of the other girls. She never came back to the club after that," DCI Chilcot added.

Hargreaves wasn't likely to forget that night in a hurry. His day had started around four AM. He had left the now well and truly deflowered girl (to his disappointment but not surprise, she wasn't a virgin) to her satisfied slumber. He was full of praise for himself, this was too good not to share. He would still have to be careful. Trust in this world meant that he had more on them than they did on him and he had let them know it. The girl could be a problem though. Hargreaves had been leading her on for a couple weeks, laying it on proper thick. When Cavendish had first sent him round to her small abode to offer some job opportunity he had been pretty fucked off. He hadn't spent the last eighteen-months give or take, licking Bobby Cavendish's pin striped arse to chase minuscule-tick-bills. Hargreaves, or Dicky as he had been known then, had expected the usual sort of girl Bobby hired. But then, Emily had opened the door and he knew then what the fuss was about. This girl didn't look like she belonged in Bobby Cavendish's world. She had a natural beauty that was stunning, but her innocence made a man feel like he still stood a chance. Hargreaves had no respect for women, his mother made sure of that. He treated the opposite sex as if they were a different breed with a single purpose.
There had been an incredibly rare feeling in Hargreaves, it was enough to make him want to try. All of that ended abruptly, however. As soon as he'd shot his load inside the girl then he had known. His job here was done. Next.

Hargreaves had left the girl's pokey flat and driven back home for a few hours kip before work later that day. Cavendish had asked to see him especially. He'd needed this news for some weeks now. The budding feeling of suspicion from his superiors, his undercover contact had made that perfectly clear. It was true though, there was something to it.

He hadn't given them any significant intel of late and he himself knew what the problem was. Hargreaves loved it too much. This hadn't been his first time under cover, but it was his favourite. Bobby Cavendish was a total psychopath if you crossed him, but Hargreaves was well in with him. He was confident that if he could find a way to disappear out of the police force, he could take over Bobby' business in a year or two. Once he got rid of those heavies then Cavendish was just one man. Then he would get him. Of course, all that was fantasy. But it hadn't stopped Hargreaves from putting a nice little nest egg of cash away, in a different name than his own (or his cryptonym). You never know what the future might hold.

Right then, Hargreaves was feeling very good. He was on his way across the city to carry out the job Bobby had trusted him with. The meeting with Cavendish had gone well. He had even been invited up to Cavendish's penthouse, the flat above the club he had spared no expense on. Cavendish had offered him a seat and made Hargreaves comfortable with his warm and welcoming manner. They made small talk before Cavendish had got down to business. The job itself was simple enough, Hargreaves would just be there as a face for the drug transaction. Clearly Cavendish thought enough of "Dicky" to ask him to represent the business. There was more though. After the deal had taken place, Cavendish wanted Hargreaves to "take care" of the dealer. It had to happen after the deal so Hargreaves could follow him to his private address. Ordinarily this might have been a problem. The incident with Mark Ross aside, he wasn't what you would call an assassin. That wasn't to say he wasn't capable of cold-blooded murder. There were many times he had wanted to in his life. In the end though, it was the cancer that got his mother. But none of that mattered now as this was an opportunity for him to satisfy both his employers at the same time. He had no intention of killing the dealer at all. He would threaten the man using any means necessary but just as the career criminal sensed his time was up and begged Hargreaves for mercy, that's when he would offer the man a way out. There was no doubt a ton of information this kingpin of the heroin business could offer to keep the organised crime unit at bay. Bobby Cavendish would be none the wiser.

The routine drug deal had gone swimmingly so Hargreaves carried out the second part of his duties. The man had been harder to crack than was expected, making numerous attempts to take Hargreaves' gun from him. It took a long time for Hargreaves to bring the man back around after he had knocked him unconscious, using the barrel of his illegal handgun. The man had sung to the same song sheet after that. Paul Hargreaves, having handed the badly bruised criminal over to his undercover contact "Doris", decided he would celebrate. He didn't fancy going back to the club again, having already had his fill of Dee earlier that day. Cavendish had insisted on racking up some lines for the two of them after the business side of the meeting was over.

Hargreaves was so charged up he had to let out some steam once he left the private upper floor. Dee had been a natural choice. "Dirty bitch will do anything for a free whiff," he thought. He had so much fun at the time he completely lost track. Lucky, he hadn't seen Emily though, she would have kicked off for sure. He would have to be clever about it.

The girl was obviously in love with him, but then he couldn't blame her. With his mind made up and with no reason to think she wouldn't welcome his unexpected arrival. Hargreaves drove to Emily's flat.

DCI Chilcot had left Hargreaves to his thoughts for a few minutes, eyeing him contemptuously from over the table. The senior officer was clearly allowing him to mull over the story for himself, letting Hargreaves suffer on his own recollection of how it had all gone so wrong. But now Chilcot interrupted his chain of thoughts.

"I don't suppose I'll ever find out exactly what happened that night Hargreaves," Chilcot spoke his name as if it caused him a physical disgust.

"I learnt a lot through fellow officers and the many scumbags who were all too happy to divulge as much as they could about "Dicky Farrell", all of them trying in vain to help their own pitiful existences. I had toyed with the idea of torturing it out of you myself, but I know enough to justify my own actions and it's just not in me these days. All I want is closure for my family. Carry on Sergeant Paul Hargreaves, let that twisted mind of yours reflect on the biggest mistake of your life. Drink it up while you can, if there is even a tiny shred of remorse in that grey matter of yours then everything you forced me to do to get you here has been worth it."

Tears flickered in the DCI's hate filled eyes. He stopped talking again clearly allowing Hargreaves to recount the night in question.

The sergeant couldn't do it, he could see how bad it looked on him, even if he wasn't aware of what a sick fuck he was. He had always played his life out as the victim, justifying his actions by the hard treatment of his own childhood. At no point in his life had he considered what anybody else on the receiving end of his vindictive hand had been through, until now at least.

Hargreaves had finished the girl off, strangling her to death with his bare hands. She hadn't put up much of a fight, the coat hook that hung out of the back of her skull having been her true demise. He didn't need to be a doctor to see that for himself. He had not taken any pleasure from her death. The adrenalin and fear caused by the almighty fuck up had literally reduced him to tears as he sat straddled over the limp body. The tears weren't for the girl but purely towards his own current predicament.

Chilcot was looking at him with a manic satisfaction as tears ran down Hargreaves' face and fell onto the table adding to the syrupy drawl. Chilcot fixed his gaze upon him, apparently satisfied, for now he finished the story for him.

"The next time anyone saw Emily was when her body was discovered by an unfortunate family who were taking a boat trip out in the gorge. Strangulation and serious head trauma. Nobody had even reported her as missing. I understand Cavendish has a high turnover of girls; you must have been thanking the heavens when you heard the police were pinning it on Cavendish. Nice try by the way. But revealing your identity to Mr Ross' ex-partner, Keith Barwick wasn't the smartest move. He didn't trust you at all and went straight to the top brass with your attempts to frame Bobby for Emily's murder."

There wasn't much Hargreaves could do now. He knew his fate. Would he do anything different if he could do it all again? No. Probably not. If it wasn't for him, she would have suffered far worse sooner or later. She'd got off easy when he thought about it. Once Cavendish got his hands on her and then got bored, the suffering would have been far more painful. How was he supposed to know she was the legendary

DCI Chilcot's beloved niece? If only she had just played along, he may have even set her up in a little bedsit somewhere, once he had taken Cavendish down. His own little seedy secret. Sex on tap.

"I expect you hadn't bargained for Emily having such a dedicated family hey, Paul? Well, I asked you earlier what a decent cop or a committed journalist could find out didn't I?"

Hargreaves supposed he couldn't argue when the chief put it like that. Still, the boys in Bristol had his back, didn't they? Even Phipps seemed easier on him than he thought he would be. Maybe there was something in that.

"It wasn't by coincidence that you found yourself here officer. I am the reason you are not in prison right now."

Hargreaves tried to gurgle a response; it was no use.

"I told you I would induct you into our community and I think we have just about reached that time."

And with that, Paul Hargreaves lost consciousness.

THE WINNING SCARECROW

Paul Hargreaves woke up disorientated and fuzzy of mind. As he tried to collect his thoughts he took in the current surroundings. The sun was out beating down onto the grass in front of him, he could just about make out some concrete blocks sticking up out of the earth like a huge set of grey teeth. It dawned on him that they were gravestones.

Hargreaves looked out over the piled slate wall that was so typical of this part of the country. Two little boys were staring up at him with presumably their mother walking up behind them. Hargreaves recognised the mother as the lady he had seen yesterday in the town. The one who had come to the pub to report the missing scarecrow. It saddened him to think he wouldn't be getting into her knickers. The boys were excitedly pointing and talking about Hargreaves.

"This one's really good Mum," one of them said wide eyed.

"It looks real to me! He just moved his eyes Mummy!" the other lad proclaimed.

"Oh, don't be silly Johnathan. You can't see the eyes through those sunglasses its wearing, stop trying to scare your brother. This is DCI Chilcot's offering. He always does such a good job. Every year for reasons I can never understand someone steals one of the town's scarecrows, but he always finds a better one to replace it with. He really is a pillar of the community!" the mother said with obvious pride.

Hargreaves still couldn't move his body or speak. The paralysis was much worse than it had been back in the pub. His mind was beginning to put the pieces of the puzzle back together again with increasing dread for his wellbeing. As all the details of the previous day's activities came back to him, he remembered one morsel of information he hadn't linked at the time. Chilcot's wife had been paralysed temporarily. Could the chief somehow know what her ex-husband had used on her? It seemed possible. It had only taken a couple of days for it to wear off. Maybe this was just the DCI making a point to Paul. He could only hope.

"Come on boys, we can come back tonight and see it again after the judging has been done," the mother ushered her two boys along.

The family walked away along the church wall and out of Hargreaves' limited view. The ill-fated sergeant started to frantically work out a plan to get out of there, but the more he tried to move the more fatigued it made him. He didn't remember losing consciousness again.

***

"Wake up Sergeant!... Paul!"

Hargreaves' eyes slowly cracked open letting in the evening sunset along with the terrifying reality he now found himself in. The DCI stood in front of him only a few feet away, maybe he was going to let Paul down now he had learnt his lesson? Paul hadn't learnt his lesson though, if he got out of this then he would kill this old cop and anyone in this town who had anything to do with it. All because of some little whore who couldn't learn her place and keep her trap shut.

Paul's biggest regret was not making her suffer more. That and not being able to be a bad-boy gangster.

A couple of weeks after he had dumped Emily's body, Hargreaves had received a phone call from his undercover contact telling him to stand down and to come back in. They had found a girl's dead body and they thought they had enough to pin it on Bobby Cavendish. He had been more than disappointed to learn his fun in the criminal underworld had come to an end, but he hadn't been surprised about Bobby. After all it was Hargreaves himself who had called it in, along with the information he'd given Keith Barwick. He had put a lot of work in to frame Cavendish for the girl's death. Returning to the flat to plant his boss' DNA, as well as making sure the girl had a business card of Cavendish on her person. There would be witnesses that could confirm she had worked at the club too and if the police were quick enough, they would have the CCTV footage. The contents of which had led to his current demotion. He hadn't seen it himself, but he was grateful of the privacy the private rooms allowed. Some of it had been leaked to the press, they were currently sitting on it, only due to the dangerous position it could leave Hargreaves in with Bobby's associates. At least that's what his superior had told him... So why was he here? He had been so sure that he'd covered all his tracks.

"I knew you'd make a fine contribution to the town's community Sergeant," Chilcot said quietly.

He was standing right in front of Hargreaves now. No one else seemed to be in the street or graveyard. Did that mean no one else knew he was tied up here if the DCI was keeping quiet, he wondered.

"A fine scarecrow you make Hargreaves. Certainly, better than you were at being a police officer, or a human being for that matter."

Chilcot stood back looking at the fully clothed scarecrow. It really was a fine job. No pumpkin head or straw hands. Paul's face was covered with a balaclava and large straw sun hat pulled down low over the top of his head. Green oversized wax gardening gloves concealed his hands as did wellies on his feet. DCI Chilcot had stuffed the blue overalls well with straw, so much that it made Hargreaves look incredibly bloated (but perhaps worth it, thought the DCI). After all, it made it very hard to notice Hargreaves' chest beginning to puff in and out. so panicked was his breathing. The wooden cross staked into the ground held him fast, as did the rope tying him to the frame. Dark sunglasses covered his eyes.

"You know what Sergeant? I think you even make a better offering than Dennis Carter did in Maggie's Garden all those years ago. Such a shame we couldn't get our hands-on Michael Dawson's body. Unfortunately, as you know, I was away and unaware at the time, it would have made such a fine show piece in my wife's garden too. Never mind, at least Michael's vial of medicine came in use. I always knew it would. Thankfully the police never did find it after they searched through the atrocities carried out at my darling Alice's house. But she did. Don McKay was kind enough to keep it at his for me in an old whiskey bottle. I can't wait to show her how well it has worked. It's much better in lots of small doses than all in one go, as we learnt last night. Alice loved Hannah like a daughter Paul, I think I shall let her light the first match…"

Hargreaves did… well nothing. He couldn't react at all.

"Oh. Did we not tell you? We always burn the scarecrows after the judging is complete. How else would we stop people from entering the same one every year? Mrs Wells insists I'm afraid," Chilcot said before dropping his cheery outlook and replacing it with a cold intense stare. He was inches away from the sergeant's face now, staring up at him with the same soul-searching look he had given him on their first meeting. Hargreaves could smell the stale beer on Chilcot's breath reminding him of the ale that had got him into this state.

"They won't miss you. No one misses you Hargreaves. I told you, Phipps and I go way back."

"Bollocks!" Hargreaves wanted to scream. No way would they turn on him, he was the best at what he did. Everyone respected and loved him too much to not have his back. Didn't they?

"Your body will be found in Bristol's Down's. Far too badly damaged to be identified through visual means but have no fear, Paul! Your body will receive a decent burial, though the police records will claim that it is in fact that of Robert Cavendish".

Hargreaves desperately hoped he had misheard, maybe the DCI was going to let him go after all, he kidded himself. But sadly, for Paul Hargreaves the chief hadn't finished talking.

"Mr Cavendish has been ever so helpful you see Paul. He was instrumental in uncovering the truth that has led to your being here today. It seems Bobby Cavendish had quite a liking for Hannah. I'm not sure if I would have approved of him as a potential suitor, but I suppose that's beside the point now. Giving a man such as that his freedom would usually leave a bitter taste in my mouth. But Robert Cavendish will be found dead and Paul Hargreaves will leave the police force. I have made my peace with that."

Hargreaves noticed that the experienced cop looked troubled by this. Was he really worse than Bobby Cavendish? If he could speak then he might have tried to dispute this. But then again, Cavendish hadn't killed the DCI's niece, and he really couldn't argue with that.

"How you ever made it as police officer still astounds me. Personally, making myself aware of all of Cavendish's camera system would have been my priority as an undercover policeman. I mean he literally has them everywhere, as I understand it. What your biggest faux pas was and the reason why you aren't currently being subjected to one of Bobby Cavendish's more inventive death sentences is the details you gave Keith Barwick. That allowed Hannah's body to be discovered, a small piece of unintentional closure you allowed my wife and me. However, it also led to your downfall as with Hannah's body now discovered, Mr Cavendish knowing he hadn't done it himself could think of only one other person to investigate. With the trail of ignorance that you left in your wake I hear it wasn't hard. It didn't take all that much really. The suspicions were already there, but his camera surveillance allowed us all to confirm your whereabouts both on the night of her murder and the subsequent days that led up to your tip off. Regardless of whether Cavendish's business tastes were to my liking, I cannot take away from the fact that he ran his empire better than most politicians run the country. Cameras weren't all he had available to him. Naturally, he had his own police contact to warn of the impending arrest and acted fast. It was indeed perfect timing that put him into my lap. We all have Alice to thank for that Paul. Both Bobby and I had something each other wanted and the same common goal. That is why he will now be going free as Paul Hargreaves and you will be dying as Robert Cavendish."

Chilcot stopped to wave at some of the fellow villagers in greeting. Hargreaves despite his impending doom still had to appreciate the humour of the situation. He had wanted nothing more than to be Bobby Cavendish, just not like this and now he found himself not laughing but crying. He strained to see through his tears at the milling crowds passing by to see him. Every one of the town's people staring and complementing DCI Chilcot's fantastic handiwork for making such a convincing scarecrow yet again. After shaking some hands and receiving thanks he turned back to Hargreaves.

"These scarecrows don't make themselves Paul and there is one that always seems to go missing just before the event. Lucky the town have me hey?" DCI Chilcot looked at Hargreaves one more time with what seemed like sadness, or regret, before leaving him to join a group of chirpy villagers.

Couldn't they see he was alive? he screamed to himself. The former police sergeant knew his time was running out. The crowds of spectators began to ebb away to the less frequent visitor.
Hargreaves willed his arms to work, sent messages to his legs but it was no good. Even if he could get some mobility back it wouldn't be enough to break through the rope restraints. Exhausted from trying to will his limbs to move, he soon passed out.

The sun had completely set, giving way to darkness, when DCI Chilcot returned. He removed Hargreaves' sunglasses exposing terrified bloodshot eyes. Behind the church wall standing in the street were the town's residents each holding their own flaming torch. Their faces danced with the shadow and illumination of the wavering flames. As menacing as the image was it also gave Hargreaves some hope. Surely Chilcot wouldn't risk killing him with so many witnesses? Maybe the old boy had changed his mind about ending his life or was it just a threat from the beginning and here he was to let Hargreaves go after learning his lesson? Given half a chance he could definitely pretend he was sorry. But only until he got out of this carrot crunching town. Unfortunately for him, he would have no such luck.

Chilcot seemed to read his thoughts. "Oh yes, I think Mrs Chilcot will enjoy this very much. If it wasn't for my wife, we would have never found you." He looked back as a lady came up towards the graveyard holding her own torch. Hargreaves noticed she had a limp and as the woman drew closer, he could make her out as the badly dressed woman from outside of Cavendish's club. It all made sense now, even the brilliant Paul Hargreaves had to admit this had been an almighty fuck up on his part. He noticed another figure standing alone by the church wall but couldn't yet work out their features.

"Hello Dicky Farrell, we never did get to meet. I'm Alice Chilcot." She forced a smile at Hargreaves before chucking her torch down between his legs. Alice kissed Chilcot on the cheek which he returned with a loving squeeze of her arm before she headed back towards the street. Hargreaves looked down as much as his position would allow him. The fire from the torch was beginning to singe the hay extending from his oversized trousers but nothing had caught fire yet. Before he could make sense of it another familiar figure walked up towards him also holding their own flaming torch.

"Hello Sergeant, how lovely to see you again. Don't worry about your car it's in great hands! My brother, Jon, runs the local scrap yard," Donovan McKay beamed before laying his own incendiary beneath Paul's legs. The flame joined the journalist's and grew, now beginning to scorch his trouser legs. Before the farmer had left the cemetery, another face Hargreaves wished he could forget dropped her torch with a farewell.

A shadow brushed his field of vision, not yet quite solid.

"Thank you…Sergeant," Maggie his brief hotelier smiled.

It was the next face as the flames now began to catch on his upper trouser legs that really troubled him. The girl stepped closer than anyone else had, stretching up towards his ear on her tip toes to whisper in his ear.

"Maggie found my knickers you dirty cunt!" Millie spat out the last word and dropped her torch with a `drop the mic` gesture that would have made Freddy proud. The farmer's daughter was replaced by Harry, The Ivy Tavern's landlord. *Her face, as it was, again*. He blinked it away. By this point the fire beneath Hargreaves was up to his groin, the heat from the flames drying the moisture from his eyes. It was impossible to hear the other local's words as they continued to drop their torches upon the increasing inferno roaring around him. People came and went, dropping their torches. The two lower ranked coppers from the pub he recognised but most of the others he had never seen before. With the extra hay stuffed in and around the scarecrow's overalls the flames danced up his body engulfing him in flame. *She floated closer towards him, their eyes meeting.* Hargreaves felt nothing, barely even the smell of his life and body burning. Just before Hargreaves lost consciousness, he watched the final torch dropping from her hands as *She* stood between him and the flames.

"Thank you, Dicky."

EPILOGUE

Bobby Cavendish stood in line with everybody else waiting for the boarding gates to open. It was an insult to his own being, standing amongst the peasants! 'Readying-themselves' for all-inclusive seven- day holi-days. Sun seekers (ironic the thought, most of them had no doubt saved up their discount tokens from the namesake tabloid) taking a break from the monotonous grind of their boredom. *You are one of them now Bobby, old chap! If you can't beat them...* Wait! That would not be advisable, even if he could stomach mixing with 'the plebs'. His 'orders' had been strict. Keep yourself to yourself, use Hargreaves' passport to get to Spain and after that politely fuck off and don't give us a reason to find you. HA! As if they would! Chilcot and Phipps were probably more concerned about their own rear ends than his. Still, not worth blowing his cover over it, against the grain and grassing on every one of his former associates, it wouldn't just be police he was hiding from.

Bobby resented the deal. Phipps made him the offer that would be very difficult to refuse – Bobby had very sensitive skin, cheap prison soap would be the death of him without the closure he so dearly wished for, the decision, no the decision was easy for *him*: Freedom was almost worth the trade to see the light go out in Dicky Far... Paul Hargreaves' eyes. He hadn't even been allowed to attend his darling Emily's funeral. How could Bobby mourn her without this final goodbye? But of course, that had been a lie too! Her real name, as he now knew, was Hannah. Bobby just couldn't believe the lengths of trickery that those closest to him had gone to, just to pierce his heart.

The docking gates opened, a man in his early twenties announced the news to the waiting travellers. Bobby took offense with the lad's flamboyant manner. Ordinarily he would have taken it upon himself to warn the member of the airport staff to *stop mincing about* but doubted the advice would be well received. Bobby feared for society in the face of political correctness. This was no time for unwanted attention he reminded himself, so instead, Bobby Cavendish followed in single file through the boarding bridge with everyone else. A wolf among sheep.

Bobby took the seat between a large elderly lady resembling Giles' 'Grandma' and a spotty late teen who Bobby felt could do with a bloody good bath. The willpower he had shown to not gouge the cashier's eyes out over the counter, a proud achievement when he'd been told there was no first class. Oh, how he had just wanted to have some peace and quiet to grieve his beloved Emily... Hannah... No. She would always be Emily to him. As the passengers took their seats and the plane prepared for take-off, Bobby tried to imagine a new life without Emily, or any of his former associates for that matter. It was not an easy task but then, a beautiful lady – a true vision – interrupted his thoughts.

"Hello Sir, would you like any snacks or beverages from the refreshment trolley?"

He drank in the girl's radiance. So polite too. Maybe there could be life after Emily he wondered.

"No, thank you," was all he managed as they looked into each other's eyes. Bobby was slightly taken aback when the flight attendant quickly turned to the sweaty teenage boy next to him. The harlot! He watched as the ruse was carried on with numerous passengers. Well it was her lucky day. Bobby was in mourning.

***

The baggage carousel spat out endless suitcases, none of which had been Bobby's. Other passengers he recognised from the plane had picked theirs up already. There was always the chance that customs had taken an interest in him, but then spotty kid was still waiting for his too. Reassured for the time being, Bobby waited until finally he saw his suitcase coming through the flaps. Spotty kid made a move towards the carousel ahead of Bobby and grabbed a few cases.

WHERE'S

He checked them to see the name tags, threw them back.

MY

The teen grabbed Bobby's bag.

"Thank you, young man," Bobby held out his empty arms to receive the case. The 'lad' quizzed him a second, then tossed it back onto the moving belt and carried on looking for his own.

RESPECT?!!

Seizing his own bag, Bobby went to calm down at a safe distance until the spotty teen located his luggage. From there Bobby followed him along the dusty roads to a nearby cheap hotel. There would be other times to mourn. Bobby had a thing or two to teach to this kid about his kind of respect

ACKNOWLEDGEMENTS AND THANKS

First and foremost, I would like to thank everyone who has supported me along this journey. Joe Runnacles, I couldn't have even contemplated finishing this book without your encouragement, guidance and teachings. You are and always will be my Master Yoda. My beautiful wife Rendy, without you I wouldn't have had the time or courage to finish this. Thank you for your continued support and most of all tolerance. I'm indebted to all of those who took the time to read my early drafts, provide feedback and offer advice. They are Robin White, Colin Jenkins, Norman Aspin, Lauren Jenkins, Izzy Castaldo, Trevor Robinson, Colin Woodgate, Carl Best, Sam Mace, Keith Woodgate, J.M Hewitt, Rob Burgess for introducing me to the brilliant city of Bristol and so many more. Hunter and Frankie for being the most understanding children I could ever wish for. Scout for your smiles. Mum, Dad and Amber for putting up with me.

I reserve special thanks to Andrew Marsh of Dial Lane books for being a living legend. You took a chance on an unknown writer and have been a huge supporter of mine.

Thanks to Cody Sexton, EIC of Anxiety Press. Apart from your constant help and for taking on Sun Bleached Scarecrows and The Swine, The Pig, and The Porker, you showed me that book covers can be worth judging a book by.

Thanks to Alien Buddha for publishing the first edition of this novel.

And of course, Bam Barrow. My friend, partner in crime at Urban Pigs Press and proofreader. Together we've built a press that Pigs can call home.

James Jenkins January 2024

ABOUT THE AUTHOR

James Jenkins lives in Ipswich with his wife and children. He is a writer of gritty realism, dark humour and noir. His debut novel Parochial Pigs is available on Amazon and originally published by Alien Buddha Press. The sequel Sun Bleached Scarecrows is available from Anxiety Press and Amazon. The third book in the Pigs series, The Swine, The Pig and The Porker is due for release with AP in 2024. James is also the co-founder of Urban Pigs Press and can sometimes be found featuring as an editor for Punk Noir Magazine.

Follow James @
twitter.com/JamesCJenkins4
www.facebook.com/JamesJenkinsAuthor/
jamesjenkinswriter.wordpress.com/

NOW AVAILABLE FROM ANXIETY PRESS.

The sequel to Parochial Pigs.

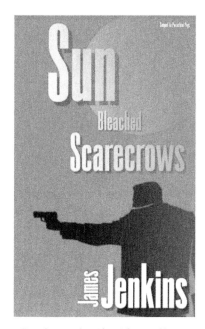

Book two in The Pigs Trilogy

AVAILABLE FROM MAY 2024

The final instalment of The Pigs Trilogy

AVAILABLE FROM URBAN PIGS PRESS

Arcanum Fabulas – Bam Barrow

Life in Dirt – James Jenkins

The Hunger Anthology in aid of FIND Families in Need – Multiple authors.

urbanpigspress.co.uk

Printed in Great Britain
by Amazon